I'm Getting Married to Mothman

I'm Getting Married to Mothman

Mothman in Love Book 3

PAIGE LAVOIE

4 Horsemen
Publications, Inc.

Matthew, for loving me in all forms.

I adore you.

Table of Contents

Heather

I**'VE ALWAYS DREAMT OF MY WEDDING** day. Heck, back when I was a kid, I'd make my Barbies kiss and craft avant-garde dresses for them out of old lace trimmings and tissues. The poofier the better. When I got older, I'd flip through Pinterest and magazines and daydream about what kind of dress I'd wear. I decided ages ago that I'd have an autumn wedding, and I knew in my heart that, one day, I'd walk down a flower-lined aisle with my mom holding my arm. I'd gaze at my partner, tears in our eyes, as we prepared for our next chapter. Despite my many plans and daydreams, I never expected Mothman to be involved—especially as the person I'd fallen madly in love with—but here we are.

If the gossip blogs got a hold of this, it would be *"A BURNT-OUT INFLUENCER AND CRYPTID MEET*

IN THE WOODS, WHAT HAPPENS NEXT WILL SHOCK YOU!"

And they'd be right because true love is something I never thought I'd find out here, especially with the local forest monster.

As the two of us sip tea after a long day of final decisions, I couldn't be happier at this twist of fate. In one week, we'll be husband and wife. The weight of the titles doesn't feel restrictive or daunting. Ever since this man fell off my roof two years ago, I knew I could spend the rest of my life with him.

"I'm so happy." I sigh, taking his clawed hand in mine.

"Which is why you have been shouting at me about centerpieces for the last few hours?" His deep voice rumbles as he rubs his temple with his free hand. Okay, I'll admit, maybe, just maybe, I've been a little *much* today. However, plum and burgundy are not the same color. Of anyone I know, Moth should know this. He's spent years in the woods among nature, right?

"Babe, there is no one I'd rather shout about centerpieces with," I tease, releasing my grip on his hand to hold tight to his middle. My chin rests flat on his stomach as I watch his perfect mouth rise into a fang-filled smile. You think I'd be used to our height difference by now, but seeing him like this makes me want to call off all my plans for the night and climb him like a tree.

"Yes, that has become very clear." He chuckles. His large hands grasp my hips, hoisting me up until our lips are flush and—God, what we're we arguing about again? His mouth presses tenderly against mine. Colors. A wedding. The only thing that really matters is I get kisses like this 24/7. A giggle rises through my chest until I'm laughing and feel his smile against my lips.

"I could be *so* much less chill. You know that, right?" I deepen the kiss as his hands cage my waist, and you know what? Maybe burgundy and plum are closer than I thought…

"Mmm," he murmurs, and okay, I could also be more chill. Honestly, he's lucky we agreed on an intimate ceremony and reception, despite my overflowing Pinterest board and the pressure from both families to do something grand. When we got to making the guest list, it became clear we only wanted our close friends. Which means I've gotten to splurge on little details, like the aforementioned centerpieces. I get the dreamy autumn aesthetic I've always wanted, Moth gets a quiet affair, and most importantly, we both get a partner for life. Plus, Holly has smuggled over half of our decor from the fae realm. I think she's still trying to make amends with me for trying to break Moth and I up last year, which has honestly been pretty cute. Of all the sisters-in-law I could have ended up with, I'm glad to have Holly. Sure, she's still a little stabby, but I think the two of us are finally becoming friends.

Glancing up at the clock, I untangle myself from my cryptid fiancé and make my way toward the door. Holly will be here any second to take Rosie, Clara, and me to the bachelorette party she's spent the last few months planning, which means they'll all start arriving any minute now.

"I know I've been a little nitpicky." I sigh, turning my attention back to my husband-to-be. "But I just want it to be perfect."

A sympathetic smile crosses Moth's face. His concern for the aesthetics of our wedding day may not be as strong as mine, but he still understands how important all of this is. After a few simple vows, he and I will be married. The whole thing should be terrifying. In the grand scheme of things, we haven't been together for all that long, but I've never been more sure of anything in my life.

I love Moth more than I ever thought possible, and I can't wait 'til I get to call him my husband.

His deep red eyes soften as he rises, pulling me tighter into his arms. Despite my tension, I melt against his body. We're in this together, all of it.

He scoops me back in for another kiss before placing me back on my feet. His clawed fingers tenderly brush a few stray hairs away from my face. "It will be everything you desire."

"Hellooo, who is ready to party?" Rosie's voice catches my attention, followed by a few knocks on the door.

"The humans have arrived." Moth sighs, leaning down to rest his forehead against mine. With his height, it must look comical.

"Probably shouldn't call your friends 'the humans.'" I stick my tongue out before heading to the door.

He grumbles, and I catch a hint of something underneath the grumpy expression I can't quite put my finger on. He might be getting more comfortable around Rosie and Clara, but even after all this time, it feels like he's holding back on our double dates. Hopefully, one day, he can fully be himself around more people than just me.

"Soon I'll be all yours," I say, fluttering up to a quick peck on the cheek.

"You are already mine, and I am yours," he whispers, tenderly stroking the length of my face before retrieving a dramatic cloak from the rack by the door to drape over my shoulders. "But yes. In just a few days it will be proclaimed in front of everyone."

I laugh. He's always so serious. When I open the door, falling leaves cascade from the trees in red and burnt orange. They shower upon my friends' heads, who all appear to have simultaneously arrived.

Holly stands stiffly between the couple, and honestly with their loud hair color and style, it's hard to tell who's a human and who's a faerie without the wings.

"Are you ready for your hen party?" Clara says, looping an arm in mine, as the trio guide me down the steps of the wraparound porch and into the woods.

"Was I supposed to procure birds?" Holly stops in her tracks, her face suddenly a ghostly shade of white.

"You *forgot* the hens?" Rosie gasps, placing her hand on her chest. I watch Holly's face go blank as she straightens, puts her heels together, and nods with the determination of a soldier.

"I will remedy this at once," she says, rushing off to God knows where.

"Holly, wait! No, they're kidding!" I shout after her, laughter overflowing from us at her bewildered expression.

"So, no birds?" my future sister-in-law asks, tilting her head.

"No birds." I nod. "I'm sure whatever you've prepared is perfect." *And preferably doesn't involve swordplay.*

"Enjoy the evening." Moth comes down the steps to steal one more kiss I will happily give. His lips taste like worry and wanting—the need to keep me close, but the knowledge that sometimes, we have to spread our wings separately.

Sprout has followed us down from the house. His fur has gotten so long and fluffy he appears to be floating like a dark cloud down the steps. As per usual, he's walking closely at my heels. The two of us have become pretty inseparable in the past year.

"Sprout, watch over Heather," Moth commands, reaching down and gently patting his head.

"*Arf!*" Sprout sits at attention as if he's a guard dog and not a oversized marshmallow.

"You trust a dog over me?" Holly whines, crossing her arms over her chest.

"Yes." After what she pulled when we first arrived in Eclipsica, I can't say I blame him. I may have forgiven her for trying to break us up, but I'm not sure Moth has let his guard down.

"I'll be home soon," I say, letting my wings unfurl and fluttering up to give him another kiss—a good one this time. You'd think after the dozen exchanged in the past few minutes, one of us would be sick of it, but when it comes to Moth, I only want more.

"So, where did you park?" Clara asks, looking up and down our driveway for Holly's car, because of course my human friends are going to assume we're taking a logical mode of transportation and going to a run of the mill venue for my bachelorette.

But there's nothing ordinary about the night Holly has planned, at least I can guess that much, the details are supposed to be a surprise.

"Oh, um," I exhale. How exactly am I going to explain this? Holly leads us deeper into the woods until we reach the shining gold spot in the hollow of a large tree.

"How do you feel about spending the night in the faerie realm?" I ask.

I had no idea what to expect when Holly took charge of my bachelorette party, but this is beyond perfect.

The east side of the castle houses a well-maintained garden with hedge mazes—actual hedge mazes! Not only is it the dreamiest backdrop for a party, but you can almost hear the echoes of drunken escapades from the past with every step. I imagine faerie royals chasing each other through the overgrown hedges of the maze, drinking wine, and having the time of their lives. Best of all? Now we get to add to the gorgeous memories.

My buttery yellow dress spills out of the dainty white garden chair, and the smell of lavender punch and faerie wine practically sings through the air. Holly has spared no detail, making sure the tables are lined with allergy-friendly treats. She even dressed to theme in a light-colored periwinkle dress that matches her hair, a breastplate with butterflies etched into the silver over top.

She hands me a cone of rose candy floss with a look of uncertainty on her usually stoic face.

"I love this so much," I say, taking a bite of the cloud-like candy and letting the honeyed taste of flowers melt across my tongue. Incredible. Reason 1001 for not making assumptions about people. I never thought Holly would pull off such an amazing and *thoughtful* garden party.

"Mother helped me with the decorations. To say I achieved this on my own would be untrue," Holly admits, casting her eyes downward while her feet shuffle almost nervously, "But I am glad this makes you happy."

Happy is an understatement. I'm overjoyed, but also relieved. I half-expected a night of ax throwing and dueling. Instead, she's fully customized this night for me. Best of all, most of my very best friends are here.

Ruby, who looks like a literal star dressed in silver sparkles, the gown beautiful against her dark brown skin. She greets us at the portal with hugs and a warm introduction to our human party guests. Widow shut the dress shop down for the night just to come celebrate.

Sure, Rosie and Clara are … understandably shocked about the whole portal travel thing. They spend the first thirty minutes whispering, "What the fuck?" which, like, honestly, is *so fair*. Thankfully, they're adjusting, I think. Widow whisking them away and offering them clothing samples to "match the theme" certainly is helping. Still, they mouth the words "What?" to each other now and then—which seems like an improvement, so I'll take it.

Now we're all in pastel colors, and despite the human realm being in the thralls of autumn, it's nice to enjoy a night that feels like spring, we even adorn Sprout with a yellow ribbon so the two of us match.

Together, we sip alcoholic and non-alcoholic drinks, while listening to one of Rosie's killer Spotify playlists. Holly even hired Oak to paint our portrait, and considering no one can stop giggling, that might have been a terrible idea.

"You may together be the embodiment of a lovely bouquet of flowers, but you are absolutely the worst group of models I've ever seen," he huffs, setting down his paintbrush. "I beg you: *stop moving*."

His frustration makes the giggles worse. I've been sticking to the punch for fear of a flare-up so close to the wedding day, and clearly don't need booze for the sillies to kick in.

"Oh, here!" Rosie says, handing him her cell phone. After a quick tutorial on how to use the camera, Oak captures our picture in an instant, and I promise to have it printed so he can use it as a reference if he ever wants to finish the painting.

"Such technology is certainly a novelty here," he says wistfully, giving me a look I pretend not to see. There are things Oak and I have talked about in the past year that I don't want anyone else to hear—or, frankly, discuss tonight.

"You are truly having a good time?" Holly asks, snapping me back to the present, blissful moment. "I conferred with our chefs to make sure nothing would trouble your diet, and since you enjoy photographs, Moth suggested the backdrop and portrait—I did not plan for music or games, so I am thankful for your humans."

"Holly, seriously, relax. It's perfect." I pull her into a hug, and she stiffens against me; we've come a long way since the drama of last year, and though she still has some walls up, it's nice to see her trying. I just wish she would worry less. Holding a grudge against her is impossible, even if I wanted to.

"Okay, games!" Clara rummages through her purse, pulling out a stack of papers and pens, passing them out to each of the guests. She is still a little jittery, but she seems to have finally gotten comfortable. The suit she's wearing is covered in peonies in deep blue, and considering most of the time I see her she's wearing overalls, it's cute the way she twirls, letting the coattails billow as she walks.

"Oooh, I have wondered what kind of games mortals play at these affairs," Oak says, ditching his post to lounge on a picnic blanket between Ruby and Widow. With the grace of a cat, he rolls on his stomach, propping up his head with his hands. "What will the stakes be?"

"Oh, well…" Clara holds up her own paper to show the group "It's a *mystical* thing called a survey, one of those 'who knows the couple best' kind of things, and the prize…"

"A cluster of gemstones?" Ruby asks, a competitive gleam now flickering in her eyes.

"A satchel of gold?" Oak offers. I note, with a smirk, that he seems to be sitting *awfully* close to everyone's favorite seamstress. They would make a cute couple.

"The blood of our enemies?" Holly asks, and everyone roars with laughter. Well, everyone except for Clara, who gives me a wide-eyed look. I shake my head and lip the words, "*She's joking.*"

"Close!" Rosie chimes with a wicked grin. "It's a gift card to a local coffee shop."

My lovely gaggle of faeries tilt their heads in confusion while I stifle a laugh. Considering we live in the middle of nowhere, my sweet neighbors had to drive upwards of an hour to get that little piece of plastic. It's not a gift to be taken lightly.

"Sounds like the winner gets a field trip to the mortal realm," Oak announces loudly.

The group erupts into chaos before straightening up, as if they're ready to take a college exam and spent the entire night studying.

"She is my future sister-in-law," Holly sneers. "I will win and have this adventure."

"Well, she's our best friend," Ruby says, wrapping an arm around Oak, ever-so-slightly pulling him away from Widow, who I notice is now wearing a frown on her bright red lips. "We will be formidable rivals."

"Not so fast!" Rosie argues, not so quick to give up the fight. "She's *our* best friend too, and playing as a team is not allowed."

"Okay, you are *all* my best friends, so calm down," I say with as much authority as I can muster. Honestly, how can I pretend I'm not loving this? A few years ago, I could easily count my genuine friends on one hand, and now I'm surrounded by these wonderful people, and they're fighting over me! This may be one of the best moments of my life—until the wedding, of course. I love them all so much.

"Question one!" Clara announces. "How did our happy couple meet?"

"Oh, that's easy: he fell on her roof," Rosie replies—*loudly.* Everyone scribbles down their answers with smiles across their faces.

"Shh." Clara shakes her head. "Do you want to win this or not, babe?"

"Sorry!" She laughs. "Ignore me." And if the others want to win, I hope they ignore her. Technically, Rosie is incorrect—but, by the smug expression on Holly and Ruby's faces, it's a detail I don't think they remember as they copy Rosie's answer.

"Wrong! Heather fell out of a tree and Moth saved her," Clara announces, placing a hand on her hip as if she knew all along and the answers aren't written on the card in front of her.

"How romantic! Why don't you ever tell that part of the story?" Ruby asks, casting her amber gaze in my direction.

"Because I thought he was going to kill me."

"Ah, people love a twist—leave it in next time," Clara teases, shuffling the deck of cards, gaining a look of approval from Holly. "Okay, second question! Where was their first date?"

"That grubby little diner you took me to on my last visit!" Holly replies with her head held high. If she managed to pay attention to the rules, she might actually win this thing.

"You're going to need to write down the answers if you want to win," Clara reminds her, pressing a hand to her forehead. "Who said 'I love you' first?"

Me. I don't mention that I shouted it during a fight, but whatever, it still counts.

"Who is messier?"

Honestly, that's a tie. We both leave coffee cups all over the house, although my clothes are normally scattered as well. Moth still hates wearing pants.

"Where will they be going on their honeymoon?"

Queen Plume offered us their summer chateau in the Butterfly Court. It's apparently in the middle of fields of flowers, totally secluded and, considering I still haven't seen much of Eclipsica beyond Moth's territory, was hard to say "no" to. Meanwhile, Clara and Rosie are trying to peer pressure us into doing a joint theme park trip in Florida for their anniversary, which Moth is understandably on the fence about. The truth is though, we haven't actually decided on anywhere, though Moth seems like he has something sneaky he's been planning.

The group shouts, writes, and debates their answers while I comfortably sit watching the chaos unfold before excusing myself to refill my lavender punch.

Oak sidles up beside me. Ugh. I guess there's no use putting this off any longer.

"Dropping out of the game?" I ask. I know he wants to talk, but I figured he'd be more competitive…

"You know I'm seeking answers of a different kind," Oak says, tapping his foot expectedly.

"Oh, come on, it's a party. *My party*," I whine. It's not that I've been avoiding him the entire party … except I have. Oak and I have been exchanging letters over the last few months. He throws one through the portal and I send one back before it closes. Unless I miss it, then I have to wait until he realizes and sends another message. Moth thinks it's nice—like an interdimensional pen pal.

The brunette faerie leans in closer to me, a hungry gleam in his eyes. "Have you told your betrothed what we've discussed?"

"The thing is…"

"Which is a 'no.'" Oak runs his fingers through his messy hair.

"It's a yes. We've talked…" I shake my head. "And it's a no. I just didn't know how to tell you because…"

Because it's all I have been thinking about, besides, of course, the wedding.

"You have mentioned the cabin like it's something you've outgrown," he grumbles, crossing his arms. "And we've talked at length about how your creativity could—"

"Oak! That doesn't mean I want to move to Eclipsica!"

He hushes me, but luckily our friends are too focused on the game to pay attention to our *very annoying* conversation.

"Clearly you have not explained our exciting business venture well enough!" he says, his amber eyes flaring. I feel badly that I've made him wait this long for an answer, but our communication has been shoddy—and a shining example of why this just won't work. Still, the idea of it makes something in my heart ache with longing.

A portrait studio attached to Widow's dress shop. It would use a mix of mortal supplies—like instant cameras, film, ring lights and other bobbles—and Oak's talent when it comes to painting. When he saw how I art-directed for Moth's portrait and my portfolio, Oak became interested in bringing me on as a partner. The few times he's visited our cabin we've made some really fun pieces too; same for whenever Moth and I visit the castle. Not only have we become great friends, but we work well together.

And the thing is, I love the idea. Sure, I'm overwhelmed by the logistics—like how do we explain bringing mortal tech to Eclipsica? A studio like this would be run-of-the-mill in the mortal realm, but here? The novelty alone would drive business to us, but also to Widow's shop, which, thanks to Queen Plume and Ruby wearing her pieces in court, is finally blooming.

"Moth said he'd support anything I wanted…"

I enjoy spending time here without the pressures of royal life—Oak knows that. Still, I'm happiest at home with Moth. It's a soft, comfortable life, but that doesn't change the fact that it feels like something is shifting…

"So then … I don't understand." Oak rocks back and forth on his heel. "You want to say 'yes,' correct? Why is it not a 'yes'?"

"Because I don't want to move here," I explain. Not when my half my friends, mom, and home would be a world away. "The magic you use for letters is—"

"Finnicky?"

I nod. Making a leap this big could change everything, and that's not something I'm willing to do. Last year, we made our choice. I'll help Oak out by giving him some equipment and whatever novelties he needs, but commuting to work with only one portal? Yeah, that's not going to work.

"But what if—"

"It's not like I can get on a bus." I sigh, shaking my head. "Oh, a bus is like a big mode of transport—"

"I know what a bus is, Heather," Oak snaps.

"Okay, well! The magic is weird, and I can't rely on you or Holly to pick me up every single day. What if something happens to Queen Plume's portal and I'm stuck here?"

The few times we've hung out, Oak is always at least two hours late. He says time runs differently in the faerie realm, but I suspect it has more to do with him losing track of time with a certain seamstress. Who, given the way she is looking at me from across the garden, absolutely knows what we're talking about.

I have been actively working on the whole people-pleasing thing. I'm not about to give in to peer pressure at my own bachelorette party!

"What I am hearing is," he begins with hope in his eyes, "if I can find some way to reliably steal you away, we can discuss this again?" I glance toward our friends. Holly stares for just a moment before returning her attention to the game.

Ugh, I need to keep it down. She would jump at the chance to have us move closer.

"Oak," I say warningly, but the ache for a new creative opportunity burns in my chest. "Look, if you did somehow figure out a way to make the commute normal, I would love to. It's just—even now, the idea of something happening and not being able to get back is terrifying. Besides, I still haven't even told my mom about all of this. I want to before the wedding, but it's just…"

"A lot?" he offers, finally seeming to understand. He lays a delicate hand on my shoulder. "Let us table this 'til after your nuptials, yes? I am sorry for my overzealous nature, but you should know that I'm ordering a sign next week. I'd like to know if I should engrave your name upon it."

"Nuptials *and* honeymoon. Look, either way, I don't need my name on a sign. I'll set you up with all the goods before opening day, okay?" I plead. "You'll make something amazing with or without me."

"I do not mean to pressure you, my friend." He perks up, shaking the crestfallen expression into something that resembles a smile. "Whatever you decide, I will support, but I truly think a collaboration between the three of us could be wonderful. I can feel the creativity ready to burst from your veins."

"Me too," I agree. "But I like my cozy life in the mortal realm too. I wish I could have my cake and eat it or whatever."

Oak opens his mouth to speak, but we're interrupted by a chorus of shrieks, clapping, and my steely sister-in-law's protests.

"I won!" Ruby shouts, rising from her seat as the party cheers.

"Not fair! She's written half of the things I answered verbally." Holly crosses her arms.

"I mean, you kinda gave those answers to everyone." I laugh, giving Ruby a thumbs up. Heck yes, if anyone deserves a day out for coffee, it's the busy mom in the group. Regarding the rest of the bridal party, I raise my mocktail into the air. "Now, who wants to run through a hedge maze?"

2.

Moth

WEDDING.

My lips quirk into a smile. For all the time wandering around this mortal plane, I never thought I would see the day. Heather has only been in my life for a short time; even still, I cannot imagine a day without her. I want to make this as special as she has dreamt of. Especially considering there are variables in our lives she never considered. She is a faerie, a bride—*my bride.*

Butterflies swell in my chest at the thought of seeing her dressed in something white with frills—my perfect confection. I am thankful she's bonded so well with a seamstress like Widow. I have ensured her favorite items have been altered to accommodate her wings. Still, neither of us mind our space well and tend to bump into things around the cabin. She seems more comfortable now, especially with access to her full wardrobe.

And though I have not been permitted to see her gown before our wedding day, I know my flame would look like a goddess in anything. I trust Widow has created a garment that will complement her perfectly.

Yes. It seems wherever my flame goes, warmth follows. She has found comfort with my family and her friendships. She acts with an ease that I find admirable, aspirational even. Often, I am teased for my standoffish nature. Brooding, grumpy, even strange. In truth, I am most comfortable when I can simply observe. Both here and in the other realm. It is only Heather I feel I can be completely myself with.

Even after denouncing my title and crown, the mere act of thinking of Eclipsica has been *challenging*, to say the very least.

My memories of what life was like come back in hazy waves, flowing into pages of a novel I am convinced I will never finish. Despite endless conversations with Heather, I have a strange feeling that my past is a dream, and there is nothing before her.

"Brain Fog" is what Heather calls it, and it certainly is fitting. My mind is a swamp and my past lost in the marshy waters.

For a moment, I stand at the window and watch my flame disappear into the woods, Sprout following close at her heels. It is odd watching her go, knowing she'll be a world away from me, if only for one night. The portal that my mother keeps under lock and key from the rest of the realm will bring her home safe, but that doesn't relieve the uneasiness when I think of her so far from my reach.

Eclipsica should feel like home, and yet this is where I'm most comfortable, despite how cramped our living conditions have become. I do not regret returning, not in the slightest, but this cannot be home forever. Not while Heather is learning to stretch her wings and hone her skills. And this restlessness is not just my own. I have seen tabs on a website called Zillow pulled up on her phone when she thinks I am not looking.

I know my flame well enough to know when she is hiding a desire. And there is no desire I will leave unmet. Smirking to myself, I turn on the electric kettle. We have a rule against secrets, but a surprise after our wedding?

I hope it will be well received.

After I pour myself a blend of black tea and rose, I put a record on the player. It is a collection of old country songs, reminiscent of the radio signals I heard when I first arrived in this realm. How domesticated I've become since hiding in the bunkers of Point Pleasant, but then again, compared to royal life, it is quite simple.

A simple, quiet night. I'll enjoy my cup of tea, the tasks laid before me, and thoughts of my love until her return.

"Knock, knock!"

I groan and place my cup down. Was a guest missing from Heather's gathering? Everyone was accounted for, or so I thought, but then again, I was distracted. I move through the cabin, finding my glamour. It's a small necklace with a charm of pearlescent gemstones. Any human would think it had been picked up at a boutique—not from the queen of the faerie's personal collection. Checking my reflection in the mirror, I am assured my wings and antennae are indeed hidden. However, faerie magic can't hide everything. There's always a tell: claws that are too long, teeth too sharp. A glamour cannot hide my bright red eyes, which Heather has easily explained away as contacts.

Moving to the door, I open it, revealing my future mother-in-law. Strange, she was not set to arrive until tomorrow. But she is here, her bags overflowing with what appear to be florals and craft supplies. *Wonderful.*

"Am I too late?" she gasps. "Honey said that the party started at 7, and my flight—well, I changed it last minute, so I hope…"

She looks at the empty house.

"They already left, didn't they?" she asks, her blue eyes large and glassy. She and Heather have had a rocky relationship but seem to have reached a healthy understanding of what it means to broadcast their lives online. Heather still deals with the repercussions of living her life in the flash of a cell phone, but as Marsha enters the house and puts her phone in the bin at our entryway, I am grateful for the growth she has shown.

I would not enjoy being *vlogged.*

"They did." I nod. Considering the woman still doesn't know the truth of my origin, I believe it might be for the best. A night in the Fae realm is a large revelation to spring on anyone.

"Well, maybe I can still catch them. Are they at that tavern or one of the girls' houses?"

"I am afraid I do not have the address."

"*How?*"

I blink, unsure how to respond.

"*Men.*" She deflates, setting her bags down in the doorway before stepping past me into the cabin. I easily lift them, carrying them the rest of the way into the house. Huh … it seems she plans on staying here this evening.

This is an interesting turn of events.

"Just as well. I don't think she wanted me to come, anyway," she says. I do not know how to respond. From my understanding, none of our elders had been invited. Holly promised a small gathering.

"I do not know if it will bring you solace, but my mother is also not in attendance."

She sighs. "I guess it's alright for her to have a night with just her friends." She shakes her head. "Not everyone wants to be sitting next to their mother at a strip club."

A what? Reflexively, my eyebrow quirks, which is apparently a laughable gesture considering the way Marsha chuckles.

"Oh, come on, you know what happens at these things." She ribs me with her elbow like we are a couple of old friends.

Apparently, I do not.

"At least let me help you with this mess." She gestures to the unfinished centerpieces as she shrugs off her large pink coat. "I'm sure she's told you how much I love a good craft project." Marsha cracks her knuckles, seemingly ready to distract herself with the mess laid before us.

Moving to throw a log on the fire, I sigh. It appears I will not be spending a quiet evening alone after all.

This will not stand.

No, such a hideous mockery of my flame's wishes cannot be, just days before our wedding. Not now, not ever. I pick one of the ribbons from the table, holding the plum strand between the tip of my claws.

"She specifically asked for burgundy," I seethe.

"Sweetie, it all matches just fine." Marsha bats away my worries with a flick of her wrist. For a moment, her hand passes through the glamour that hides my wings from sight, causing an uncomfortable tingle down my spine. My future mother-in-law, thankfully, does not seem to notice. "You need to relax."

Relax.

Hah.

Relax. So says my future mother-in-law after she's shown up two days early with the wrong color ribbon, and a hodge-podge of craft supplies I'm not sure what to make of.

How am I supposed to *relax* when the one task I was meant to complete has been bulldozed by this woman?

"Also, since when does the groom worry about any of this stuff?" She laughs. I cock my head, unable to gather the meaning from her words.

It is *our* wedding, and Heather has stressed its significance many times. I will do what I must to make it as wondrous as she imagines. Even if it means arguing with Marsha about the acceptable shade of ribbon, though I do not intend to treat her with anything other than respect. She is Heather's mother, and will soon be my family as well. But as my bride is not here to defend her vision; it is a role I must not fail in.

Marsha skillfully blends the light purple ribbons in with the dark. I blink, watching the way the colors blend into something with more depth than just the one shade itself.

Perhaps this time she is right. Heather has always commended her mother's craftiness, but it is something else to see it firsthand. Resigned, I copy the movement of her hands, weaving and tying the small ribbons around the mason jars that will eventually hold tea lights. Sure enough, they match just fine, and a small amount of tension falls from my shoulders.

"We really need to get you some more friends. Heather is out partying! You should be having a wild night with the guys, not making floral arrangements with your future mother-in-law."

"I am content with the number of friendships I have at the present," I say with a shrug. My life is more social than it has been in decades. And it is unsurprising: who would not want to bask in the glow of my flame? She seems to attract admirers and friends wherever we go, and I am happy to watch her effortlessly go into those relationships. We all have our talents. She is the light, and I am happy she joins me in the shadows each evening.

"As outgoing as ever." She laughs, tying another ribbon around a mason jar. "But you're cute. I'll give Heather that."

"Honestly, I didn't really need to come early, did I?" She rises from the table, "You two probably could handle all this before the wedding day. I never thought she'd want something so small. Then again, this whole thing came out of left field. I never thought she'd want to step out of the spotlight. I'm glad she did though…"

Words I never thought I would hear Heather's mother say.

"You are?"

"Well, yeah!" She smiles. "Who knew she'd find such a handsome man to settle down with—and crafty too!" After admiring my handiwork on the centerpieces, her gaze picks up as she appraises the large archway in our small living room. It still requires the addition of fresh flowers. Mother is having them brought in from the garden. I would be happy to get married surrounded by just the trees, but it's been touching for Heather to see everyone come together to make our day special, and I love to see her smile.

"She's happy with you," Marsha says taking on a more serious tone. "Frankly, I've never seen her so happy. Not in a long time, at least. A few missing details will not change that."

"Your daughter is everything to me."

"Good," she says. "God, I'm going to have the most beautiful grandchildren one day."

My flame has always said that her mother takes only five minutes to ruin a heart-to-heart moment. I think we nearly made record time on this attempt.

"Still, I'm surprised, these life changes are all fast for her." She shakes her head. I can understand the apprehension. Her only child is marrying a man she herself has not come to know. Marsha and I have spent very little time together. I suppose I should be grateful for the opportunity to bond with her.

"The phrase I have heard Heather use is 'when you know you know.' And I believe it is the correct sentiment," I offer, wondering how long this conversation will persist.

"But I don't even think I know your last name." She squints as if staring at me long enough will make it reveal itself to her. The name "Prince Moth of Eclipsica" would be just as strange to reveal as "Mothman."

"I plan on taking hers, mine is of no consequence," I reply easily.

"A modern man." Marsha laughs. "The invitations were pretty informal as well…"

She is clearly digging for information—a predicament indeed. Secrets will be told in time. But, it is important they come from Heather's lips. Marsha is her mother, after all.

Sprout pushes his way through the door, whining and spinning in circles, scratching at my leg—a signal for me to follow. But why? I stand. The room spins for a moment as my second form begs to burst free of the bindings of flesh.

It is possible the magic of my glamour is the only thing keeping me in this human form on my bones.

There is an urgency to his barking that makes my hair stand on end. His very presence here does not bode well, and the creature inside me begs to spread its wings.

"You will excuse me," I say—an order, not a question—and I curse myself for not having more social grace. But Marsha just laughs, telling me to take Sprout for his "walkies."

While I am glad she does not follow, the persistence of Sprout's bark as he shepherds me toward the forest makes every fear I have for my flame's safety come to the forefront of my mind.

Something is wrong.

Heather

One hour earlier.

"There is a small tradition in Eclipsica," Holly announces, retrieving a long silk ribbon from her satchel. "It is said a faerie of pure intent can make it all the way through the maze by following their heart alone. You'll be blindfolded, of course."

"That's ridiculous. Let's do it." I say. I'm not sure if it's the sugar pulsing through my veins or my eagerness to get away from the conversation with Oak, but I bounce on my heels ready to take part.

"We will also be looking for you," Holly says, a wicked laugh in her voice. "If you are caught by any of us, you'll have to start at the beginning."

"Wait, what?!" I gasp. "Who made up these rules?"

"The courts of Eclipsica, of course," Holly says. "It was much more dubious in olden times, but has turned into a children's game since called 'Marry the King.' Despite my brother's disinterest in the crown, I thought it would be a *festive* way to welcome you. Do you hate it?"

I wish she would stop worrying, there's nothing that could make tonight less perfect. That being said, I'm *so* not even going to ask what the old rules are. The more I learn about the quirkiness of the fae courts, the more I wish I could forget. With all the drama, kidnapping, and swordplay, I'm glad I ended up with a group as cozy as this.

"Of course not! I think it's sweet," I say. If anyone can face an impossible challenge like this, it's me. My love for Moth knows no bounds.

"And no one expects you to win," Ruby says as the blindfold is tightened. "The task is impossible—and all in fun."

Well, now winning is all I want to do.

"You don't think I can win?" I whine as Holly spins me in circles. When she is done, I press on toward the maze, only to hear the laughter of the group. Fuck it. Taking a deep breath, I focus on the direction my heart tells me to go. Right, then left, I'm guided by the thought of Moth alone.

Our life together—the promises we've made and our lifelong commitment.

"I'm going the wrong way, aren't I?" I say, as my body smacks into what feels a lot like the leafy wall of the maze. The laughter that roars from my friends is so loud that I jump.

"This won't take long." Holly says, gripping my shoulders. With a quick shove I'm thrust in what I hope is the right direction.

"Oh, be kind, Holly! Heather has never been one to underestimate," Widow pipes up. It is, however, possible that I've bought her loyalty with the ungodly amount I've spent on dresses at her shop.

My wedding gown included.

Despite the well-earned teasing and laughs at my expense, this is a blast. As a kid, when I watched regency movies that featured hedge mazes, they always seemed so beautiful and romantic, but step by step, I can tell this is way bigger than I could have imagined. They gave me a head start. Considering I'm not the fastest runner, I take full advantage, racing through the maze with my arms straight out in front of me, catching myself on vines and foliage. I'm sure I'm an absolute mess. My perfect yellow dress is torn at the hem, and I can feel a collection of leaves building in my hair. If this keeps up, birds are going to start thinking it's a nest.

Echoes of conversation and laughter dance through the maze behind me, and it's not until the sound of my friends has faded that I slip my blindfold off—just a peek to get my bearings. I think I've gotten pretty far… if it's in the right direction or not, well, that has yet to be seen.

The benefit of having wings is if I get lost, I can fly my way out. Though, if this is an old Moth Court tradition, it would be nice to at least *try* to get it right, even if taking the blindfold off means bending the rules a little.

Footsteps bound behind me, but before I can run, I hear barking. Sprout leaps into my arms, bowling me over with a big sloppy dog-kiss.

"Buddddy, you're on my team, right?" I ask, fluffing up his fur. "You're not going to make me start over, hm?"

He *arfs* again, nuzzling up to me, and motivation sparks inside me. With my stubborn attitude and his nose, we've totally got this.

"Anyone on our tail?" I ask as we move through the maze.

"Arf!" he barks with almost a shake of his giant, furry head. God, he could not get any cuter.

"Okay. Do you know how to get out of here?"

He wags his tail, bounding forward, and with a new-found spring in my step, I eagerly follow.

I love having a dog. Casting aside the blindfold, I follow each fluffy step until I'm sure we must be inching close to the exit. Still, my lack of faith in the traditions of the faerie realms made me a little paranoid. I filled my purse with snacks before we officially started. With the start I got, and Oak's whole thing about time "working differently" here, I'm sure no one would mean to let me get lost for days in here, but you can never be too careful.

I smirk to myself. As if Moth would let that happen. *I wonder what he's doing right now…*

A gleaming light appears in front of me, and my heart flutters.

Perfect timing, future husband.

"Mmm, couldn't stand a single night without me, huh?" I giggle, still fully high on sugar and the adrenaline of running. We've had our fair share of fun in the gardens, but never in a hedge maze. I'm eager to add this to the list. "Should I run now to make things interesting?"

Sprout tilts his head, and I cringe. Okay, so maybe now isn't the best time for a cat-and-mouse game.

"Actually, Sprout is like right here so…" I laugh awkwardly. Also, considering our friends could appear at any time, I'd rather wait until we have the hedge maze to ourselves before we get too spicy. Though, I wouldn't say no to a make-out session…

A hand extends from within the light, gripping my wrist. It's pale and smooth with clear pointed nails and a powerful grip. My blood runs cold.

That is *not* Moth's usual manicure—or his touch. Sprout growls. His teeth dig into the hem of my dress, pulling me backward as I try to shake off the grip of whoever is holding me.

"Let go!" I shout, but the grip is iron.

"I think we waited long enough," a strange voice says.

Sprout and I try to pull away, but it's no use. My dress tears, throwing me forward in a way that's so sudden, I collide with a firm—yet very unfamiliar—chest. In a millisecond, I manage to reach for Sprout, but am only able to reach the tatters of my hem still gripped in his mouth.

As the stranger and I step through the glowing golden light, a flash of red hair catches my attention.

"Heather," says a man with pale skin and flowing red hair, "it's been too long." A small smile reveals a pair of fangs. With a smirk, he takes the piece of fabric from my hands. "It was good thinking to retrieve this from that hound. You will be harder to track now."

"Who the hell are you?" I shout as the world around me grows spotty and dark.

The man in front of me freezes, before a deep frown creases on his uncannily pretty face. Somehow, I don't think that's the greeting he expected.

"Darling…" he purrs. I stiffen, as the world spins around me. "Is that any way to greet your fiancé?"

4.

Moth

APPARENTLY, PEOPLE SIMPLY DO not walk through the woods for no reason at night. I do not understand *why*—enjoying nature and the stars above, is a perfectly reasonable thing to do. But I am thankful to Sprout for providing me with an adequate excuse to slip away.

Surely, I will arrive on the other side of the portal to find Heather safely surrounded by our friends while having a wonderful, calm evening. But the shake in my limbs does not go away as I allow myself to fully transform.

I do not know what dangers I will be facing, but I will not risk being bound in something as fragile as flesh when I face them.

She is fine.

I am sure she is fine.

She *must* be fine. There are no other acceptable options.

I stomp through the castle grounds, the words as my silent mantra.

Glancing around the courtyard, it is just as I imagined it would be. Ruby sits back sipping tea from a golden mug next to Widow. While Clara chats next to her, Holly looks windswept; she combs the garden for something, her gaze finally landing on me.

"Brother—what are you doing here?" she says, her breath ragged. The mortals, who are not accustomed to seeing me in this form, gawk at first, but I do not transform back.

"Moth?" Rosie says, looking more curious than frightened at my appearance. It is not as if the humans haven't stopped over unannounced and seen me at home in this form, but I imagine it is still strange.

"Sprout alerted me there was a problem," I reply, following my sister's gaze. Everyone is scattered through the garden looking winded, but calm. Sprout, however, continues to paw at my leg. "Where is Heather?"

"That is the question." Holly scoffs, crossing her arms tight around her chest.

"You do not know?" My fists clench at her flippant response. I remind myself not to panic—what could have possibly happened within the course of a few hours? *Anything,* my mind reminds me as my vision blinks red.

"Sprout is probably calling in support to win the game." Clara rises from her seat. "I gave up half an hour ago! Heather is way too good at this."

"A game?" My voice grows sharper with every word. This world has just as many threats as ours, but with my memory foggy, the details evade me. I trust my flame, but I do not want her to be alone in a place where unknown shadows could threaten her light.

"We've been playing Marry the King in the hedge maze," Ruby explains. "Something I don't think I've done since we were young."

Recollection tugs at the edge of my mind: a young Ruby with her eyes covered, counting to ten as I rushed to hide amongst the hedges, a dark green ribbon bound across my eyes. Warm nostalgia blooms through my chest. Sometimes, Oak would join us and we three would take turns in this strange mashup of hide and seek and tag. If memory serves, we had … *fun.*

That should be all that's going on. Still, I cannot shake my worry. If it is a simple game, why would Sprout be in such distress?

"And no one has been able to find her?" I press, staring at our friends and hoping for a reasonable answer. When I am met with silence, I stretch my wings, ready to search from the air.

"Moth, that's cheating!" Ruby teases. Then, she glances up at the moon. "But, come to think of it, it has been a while…" Ruby unfurls her own wings. She glances to Oak, who is filling in the gaps of a painting that must have been started earlier in the evening. "Perhaps we should call this off…"

"Not yet. Rosie and I are still—" Clara begins, cracking her knuckles. I have seen her at game night and fear that, if the call is left to her, she will search for Heather all night.

"How long is a while?" I cut off Clara. I am barely able to focus with the way Sprout is pawing at my leg, demanding my attention. *Something is not right here.*

Heather is not known to play these kinds of tricks. If she wanted to hide and have me stalk her through the woods like a monster, all she would have had to do was ask. And she would—*she has*. She knows I would be more than willing.

"Oh…" Holly is next to glance at the moon, while the humans check their watches and cell phones. My sister blinks slowly. "It *has* … been a while," There is a wideness of her eyes that confirms something is wrong. I notice there are leaves in her hair and brambles stuck to the tulle of her dress.

"An hour-ish I think," Clara offers but seems unsure. "*Right?*"

"We were all hiding in the hedge maze and goofing around," Rosie says, breathless. I start to get the feeling that 90 minutes is a healthy underestimation. "But, but, it just kept getting later and … do you think something happened?"

Sprout barks, demanding attention. As the most reasonable member of this party, I cast my gaze down.

"What is it you are trying to tell us, my friend?" I ask. After all, he is the only one who appears to be taking Heather's disappearance seriously.

He darts into the maze, and without hesitation, I follow. The party guests race behind me, huffing to catch their breath. He runs far and fast and I worry that perhaps she has had one of her dizzy spells, and that at any moment, we will stumble across her fallen body. Compared to what I see when Sprout comes to a stop, that would have been a relief.

Sprout whines and paws at the dirt, and I can smell salt in the air. *Portal dust.* While I was worrying myself over florals and decorations, my flame was being taken right out from under our noses.

"Sprout."

He whines again, a high-pitched sound, pawing at the ground. The large ball of fluff circles around the area before finally hanging his head. Is he worried he has disappointing me?

The party guests would undoubtably still think this was a game if not for my trusted companion.

I pat Sprout's furry head, and he lets out a resigned huff.

"Well done, my friend," I say, and I feel him relax, if only slightly. I bend down to examine what is left of the portal. It is no secret that I am not well-versed in this magic, but the overpowering scent of seawater is hard to ignore. There is something slightly different to this odor than when Holly or Mother come to visit—a tang of iron in the air. The party gathers around Sprout and me, but it is only the faeries who understand the gravity of the dust that has settled on the ground.

"Remnants of a portal… one Heather seems to have been pulled though," I say, unable to fully grasp the words that have left my throat.

"I'm surprised he didn't leap in after her," Oak says, ruffling Sprout's fur in his hands. "You did a good job, boy." He continues offering the animal affirmations in a high-pitched voice until his tail begins to wag.

"It is possible Sprout could not follow." Holly leans down, pinching the dust in her fingers. "The scent of blood in the air suggests this portal has been warded."

"Warded?" I echo. I did not realize such magic was possible.

"It would mean only the person who created it can pass through," she says. "If the captor held Heather in his arms, that may have granted her access. However, we haven't answered the bigger question." Her eyebrows pinch together as she meets my eyes. "Who would want to kidnap Heather?"

Heather

*F*IVE MORE MINUTES.
That's all I want before I do any more wedding prep.

Visions from last night swim through my head. It can be stressful having friend groups mesh for the first time, but Rosie and Clara fit right in with everyone from Eclipsica. I wonder if they feel as wrecked as I do. When I stir, my legs glide across silk sheets, an unfamiliar texture that sends a jolt through my system as if I'd just taken a shot of espresso.

Where the hell am I?

Shaking off the blankets, I sit up. The yellow tulle party dress is wrinkled but still firmly in place, ripped at the hem, and Sprout is nowhere to be seen. Ugh, I hope that giant fuzzball is okay. Especially after he tried so hard to pull me back to safety. I squint my eyes shut, trying to remember just what happened last night.

There's an image of a face—red flowing hair, a hand reaching through a portal, and sadness in his voice. Whoever he is pulled me away from my bachelorette party last night, but why? I piece my thoughts together while I scan the room for clues.

The idea of passing out and some stranger carrying me here and tucking me into bed makes me cringe. Running my hands down to smooth the tulle of my yellow dress, I brush against something firm in my pocket. *My phone!* I breathe out a sigh of relief, holding the device to my chest. For all the grief it's given me, I'm sure glad to have it now. The battery icon is blinking red, and I open my contact list trying to think of who is most likely to answer. Mom would, but considering I haven't exactly gotten around to telling her about the whole faerie thing…

"Come on, come on," I whisper, dialing Rosie. I wish I could call Moth, but he doesn't have a phone; he's never needed one. I'm rarely gone and starting a family plan when we're both attached to the hip has always felt like unnecessary—until now.

A deep groan from the other side of the room makes me jump. My head snaps up as I scan my surroundings for the source. A decorative sword. A letter opener at the desk. They would all be somewhat viable weapons if I knew how to fight, but given I'm *me*, I choose the most intimidating of the three. Creeping out of the bed, I move to explore the rest of my surroundings, and then I see *him*.

Hunched in a chair, which happens to be blocking the only door, there's a man. His long red hair falls in front of a deathly pale face. This is my captor, and he's *asleep*. I study him for a moment, and though some kind of familiarity tugs at my chest, I don't think we've met.

Turning my attention back to my phone, I listen to the unanswered ring until Rosie's voicemail message plays. The battery is low, which means I don't have a whole lot of time.

"Help, I'm in some kind of—" I whisper, and again, the man with the long red hair stirs. Shit, okay, quieter… I can be quieter. "—a tower. There's a man with red hair who pulled me through a portal, and this wasn't a part of Holly's game, was it? Because I'm totally freaking out." My nerves have made me ramble. What can I tell her that's useful? The one window in this place looks sealed shut, and if my kidnapper wasn't blocking the door, I'm sure it's locked. My hairpin skills may be handy for a braid crown, but I haven't exactly added picking locks to my skillset. With the sheer number of times I've become live bait though, I really should. This guy must want something with Moth, right? Why else would he have brought me here? Still, that doesn't explain why he called me his … *fiancé*. God, this is such a mess.

While I continue to list off facts about the room, I stand on the bed to grab one of the decorative swords off the wall. This is when the man's eyes flutter open. They're purple and pretty and even more shocking, he has the freaking audacity to smile at me. *Smile!* He raises his hands in surrender. I hold the sword in one hand while I palm my cellphone behind my back.

"It is normal to be startled, but you are safe here, I promise." His voice isn't as deep as Moth's, but still rumbles through the small space.

"You pulled me through a portal!"

"Guilty, yes. Of course, you must remem—"

"At my *bachelorette party*!" I cut him off, refusing to let this asshole get a word in. Mustering all the skill I've gathered in the few lessons Holly insisted on, I point the tip of the sword directly at his throat, and oh my God, I cannot believe I'm *threatening someone* at sword-point right now.

"Well, waiting 'til the wedding would have been a tad dramatic—even for my taste." His lips raise revealing his long, pointed fangs. Compared to Moth's pointed teeth, they're barely anything to gawk at. Still, I won't be disarmed by his casual way of speaking.

I position myself the way Holly taught me. It's been months since the last time she convinced me sparring would be a fun way to bond, and now I'm just hoping that maybe—maybe—I remember enough.

"Come now, as much as I enjoy a beautiful woman threatening me…" He catches the blade with his bare hands. It's *not* blunted. A small droplet of blood spills from his palm, but his expression—that flirty, tantalizing gaze—doesn't waver.

"You can drop the act, my love." A smile on his lips. "Your so-called friends are too far to hear your cries of displeasure, and I'd rather you throw yourself into my arms."

What is he talking about?

"No doubt you've thought about this day since our last meeting. I hope you know I would have never let you marry that brute." The man pushes my sword further away from his neck while rising from the chair he had been sleeping in.

"Excuse me?" I ask, my mouth hanging open. This has got to be some kind of mistake, right? He's confused me for someone else—messed up a spell. I don't even know this guy; there's no possible way he could think I'm … in love with him? I wonder if the voicemail is picking any of this up. If it is, maybe there's some breadcrumb in his words that will lead Moth to me.

"I told you I would come for you when the time was right." He leans close so that his body brushes against mine. "I'm just sorry it took so long."

"I think you're confused."

"Sweet Heather, I have never been more certain of anything in my life."

"I don't know who you are."

"Then he has … corrupted the memory of our meeting." The man gasps clutching a hand to his chest. "Does the moth prince truly have such power?"

"Maybe you're just not that memorable," I huff before reminding myself I need to get information from him, not banter.

"Impossible."

"Try me," I say, dropping the sword so my thumbs can work the keypad of my phone behind my back. I've had the thought that I could use social media with my eyes closed. Let's hope I can send a text.

"Magnus," he says, more desperate than irritated. It still doesn't ring a bell, and the question between us hangs in the air. I blink.

Magnus…

Considering the way his fanged mouth is gaping at me the longer it takes me to puzzle this together, I guess we must know each other somehow. And though there's a vague stirring in my memory when I look at him, I can't figure out where we've met.

"King Magnus … of the vampire's domain."

Ohhhhhh. *That* guy! God, I vaguely remember him now. The last time we saw each other, he was getting harassed by a few gold-digging suitors. Sure, I helped him out, but it's not like there was any kind of flirting or … maybe that's not it at all. Maybe this is all some kind of ploy to get to Moth. It's happened once, and I'm not exactly keen on being live bait again. I do my best to type out a message behind my back relaying any information I can, but for all I know my thumb is sending cat GIF after cat GIF and I'm *so* screwed.

"You really haven't thought this through, have you?" I grumble, trying to mask my shaking limbs by looking horribly inconvenienced instead of terrified—and I am. I have no idea what I'm up against here, and the best I can do is try to bide enough time to figure it out.

"Oh, but I have." He nods. "You do not have to worry."

"No, no, because when Moth gets here, he's going to snap you in half. So whatever this is about, just drop it. You're not going to win."

"That's where you're wrong, my lady. I have taken every measure—"

"He will come for me." I take a step back. "I hate to admit it, but this isn't my first rodeo."

"But it will be your last." He reaches out to comb the strands of my hair with extended claws, and I shrink away.

"Whatever you want from him—"

"Want from him? *Again,* you are the one who is mistaken." He steps into the light of the window, tilting his head as if confused by my reaction to all of this. "I care very little of what that brooding creature wants. It is your desires that are in my best interest."

"No, dude. No way, not interested," I say, continuing to slide my thumbs across my keyboard.

"You ... *what*?"

"We met literally once!"

"*Twice.*"

"Okay and?" Does he seriously not see how problematic all of this is?

"I do not understand."

"Clearly!" I huff. "Look, I know things are different here than in the human realm but *come on!*"

"You are safe now, Heather." He reaches out as if to stroke my hair, and I back further away.

"Says my *literal* kidnapper."

"*Kidnap*—when we spoke at the ball, I *asked* for your hand." He says the words slowly, working through the puzzle out loud. "I knew the prince would not let you go so easily, so I have spent the last year planning, learning everything about my future bride while I bided my time."

I did *what* now?

No, no, *no* … he asked for *a hand*! I'm sure of it—like a favor or something. Not to literally marry him. I would have never agreed to that. I strain to remember the details of our interaction at the ball, but everything from that night is a hazy blur of brain fog and stress. There's no way I agreed to be whisked away like this.

He paces the length of the room. It's smaller than Queen Plume's tower, with dark stone and things like swords, instruments, and painting supplies stashed in the corner. It's strange. Why would he keep weapons inside a jail cell?

"No? You asked if I could give you a hand. Like, when a friend asks for a ride to the airport or help moving a couch." *Not to get married.*

"Ah, then … will you help me move this … chair?" He pulls an ornate wooden chair across the room.

"And then you'll take me back?" I ask, walking to the chair in question. It's a tufted red velvet seat he could easily lift on his own. Carefully, I slide my phone up my sleeve before lifting the chair just a little.

"And then we'll be good?" I clarify.

"And *then* we will get married." He smirks, and oh my God … I can already tell this is going to be impossible.

"I'm not helping you do shit!" I shout. Doing the only reasonable thing I can think of with the chair, I throw it at him.

"I mean, technically-speaking, you did move it," he says, lightly kicking the wooden legs with the toe of his boot. "And vulgarity suits you."

I didn't think I could hate anyone more than my first kidnapper, Chris. But *this guy* is proving to be even more annoying.

"What do you want?" I ask, throwing my arms in the air.

"*You*, Heather. I think I have made that clear."

"What … with threats, blackmail, and torture?"

"Again, this was meant to be a *rescue*." His eyes comb the length of my body, landing on the "Bride to Be" sash that hangs across my chest. He grimaces, as if realizing for the first time that it's what I've been wearing for the duration of this…rescue. "I will send for something more suitable for you to wear."

"You will *send* me back." I put my hands on my hips, and note the way my claws extend, making tiny slashes into the tulle of my skirt. "Like you just said: it was a misunderstanding. Why would you keep me here if I don't want to marry you?"

"I'm afraid that will be impossible."

Why do these paranormal folks have to be so damn dramatic?

"You get how this works, right? You kidnap me, Moth finds me, and you get brutally murdered, 'kay? Save yourself the trouble and find someone else, preferably someone you don't have to steal."

He crosses his arms, staring at the sealed window of the tower, his strong jaw set as he taps a finger on his bicep.

"And what if, this time, your prince does not come looking?" There's genuine curiosity in his voice. "This is not the first time you've disappeared now, is it?"

I flush. How does he know about that? "It's the week of our wedding."

"Your last chance to run," he counters with a click of his tongue. "People talk, sweet Heather."

"*Stop* calling me that." Only one person gets to call me cutesy nicknames, and if it's not Moth's deep voice growling "my flame," I don't want it.

"My apologies." He blinks. "But you are prone to running away when things get too hard, aren't you? I would make life so easy. You would never want to run again."

"It's not like that anymore." I say, I have a life I'm happy with—friends, a partner, a dog! People with that kind of stability don't just run... *do they?*

"And does your prince know that?"

"Yes," I answer, but there's no hiding the quake of uncertainty in my voice.

"How many days until your wedding?" he asks.

"Three," I huff. "So, the sooner you send me back the sooner—"

But he doesn't let me finish the thought, much less the sentence, before his eyes spark and he raises his chin with defiance.

"Then that is how long I have to win you over," he says in a way that makes me wonder if he's talking to me—or himself.

"That doesn't work for me!" I argue. As if I don't have a giant list of stuff to do before the wedding!

But the vampire king ignores my protest before glancing back from the doorway, his lips spread in a cocky fang-filled smile. "I don't typically lose."

Moth

MY THROAT GOES DRY AT THE word. *Kidnapped.* This is not the first time this has happened, and I swore I would never allow my flame to meet such a fate again.

Whatever is going on here in the faerie realm, it is no longer a refuge for party games and celebration. The humans must be sent home where it is safe—an idea everyone seems to be in agreement with. The party lingers in the garden while Holly and I lead Rosie and Clara to Mother's portal in the tower.

"Isn't there anything we can do to help?" Clara asks, looking a little crestfallen. Both women still wear the finery from Widow's dress shop, and I suppose there will be another bill from the seamstress in the future, but it is not of concern.

"I mean this without offense, but … what possible help could you offer?" Holly asks, as we climb the steps. Once at the top, Mother's tower is still as unnerving as it was the first day I found it. The collection of broken clocks and items from the mortal realm line the walls and shelves. My human friends are visibly tense; it is further proof that while Holly's words are harsh, they are not untrue. We do not know the threat we are facing; keeping the pair of them safe is our best option.

I cannot imagine what edge the humans could have in this situation. Then, as we approach the portal, Rosie's phone begins to buzz.

buzz buzz

buzz buzz

"I didn't think you got service over here," Rosie says, fishing the phone out of her purse.

"Heather has discovered it works best when near a portal." Holly sneers, "But might I say, it is an odd time to be—"

"It's her!" Rosie shouts, pushing her phone into my hand. I raise the screen to my eyes, reading off the series of letters.

<HEATHER:. Kemgskgagmkeglkmwew SOS HWLP VSMPIRW KPNG GOT kldmslkndalg SAFE 3 NIW. LRFY V08ceM@-. >

Hm … she is clever to have written in code, though not being able to make out the words is certainly a dilemma. As my eyes flick across the strange collection of letters, I find myself with more questions than answers.

Holly groans, casting a sideways glance at the humans. In a mere moment, her posture changes from that of a younger sister to the captain of Eclipsica's army.

"It seems you will be staying after all," she says with a resolute nod,

"Oh, good," Clara says, seeming to have second thoughts now that the decision has been made.

Rosie plays the voicemail and I cringe at the sound of cracked whispers and conversation. It cuts off before we learn anything of relevance and the room snaps into action.

We have found ourselves in the library. The books and trinkets that once lined the table are swept aside in favor of maps of the kingdom. Holly hurriedly puts pieces on a board, drawing lines between territories with a furrow in her brow. If Heather were here, she'd say something quippy like, "This is the weirdest family game night I've ever been to." But she is not—and my hands do not stop shaking without her fingers interlaced in mine.

Knowing Mother would not be keen on the idea of a large group gathered in her sanctuary, we do something equally upsetting: moving her portal down the steps into the castle. It is a larger space where plans can be drawn and will fit our rag-tag collection of humans and faeries. While Widow has returned home, Oak, Ruby and Holly bicker amongst themselves on how to proceed. Rosie and Clara play the voicemail again and again, listening for clues, and await more messages. I tirelessly attempt to decode the text message, but it is no easy task. I would expect nothing less of my clever little flame. Still, the more I look, the less it makes sense. I have written it on paper, scrambling, unscrambling, and trying to sort the code, to no avail.

"Could you decipher this?" I say, passing it to Rosie and Clara who are far more tech-savvy than I. Perhaps it is a secret language for those who communicate using devices, like GIFs or emojis.

"Oh! Got it!" Clara says instantly My theory stands correct. "It's all typos. SOS help Vampire King got me, safe for now, left voicemail—I'm sorry, y'all have vampires?"

Typo. Something I will study when the situation is less dire.

"Unfortunately, yes," Holly replies. "And it seems their king has taken a liking to Heather. If I remember correctly, Mother sat them next to each other last season. They could not have spoken more than a few times!"

"That is all it would take," I say through gritted fangs. My flame is too charming for her own good, though she might not always know it.

King Magnus…

Of course, I noticed the way he looked at her the last time we were in Eclipsica. Desire, Admiration, *Interest.* Though jealousy had turned my blood molten, I could not blame the poor fool. When in the presence of a goddess, how can one do anything but worship her? But this… this will not be forgiven.

"He summers at an estate in the Dragonfly Court," Holly says, placing a piece down on the map. "His mother was of their court, but if he is in his own domain that will be … tricky."

"Does he have any faerie abilities?" Ruby asks. "I am fairly versed in the gossip of the Moth Court, but … vampires cannot typically do things like fly. We should know what we are up against."

"Unknown." Holly paces. "We will need to gather intel. Mother will know if any missives have come, and, yes, Pepper's expertise will be needed."

"Missives?" My head spins. Why wait? My claws scream for blood and the feel of her skin. Sprout sits on top of my feet as if to prevent me from springing into the air.

"It would not be uncommon to receive a ransom," Ruby explains, giving my hand a light squeeze. "It will be okay."

"Can we circle back to the 'tricky' thing?" Clara asks. "Why would it be harder to get to the vampires than the … uh, dragonflies?" She shoots me a pleading look, as if asking me to explain. I can do nothing but shake my head.

"Their castles are deep in the shadows, of course," Holly says, gesturing across the map. "Not only do they ward their lands, but shadows move with the moon; they exist everywhere and nowhere and cannot be reached without a portal or invitation."

"Oh, the shadows. *Of course.*" Clara's blinks her eyes feverishly and eases herself into the nearest chair. I do not believe she is coping with this well, but then again, neither am I.

"I thought vampires were the ones who had to be invited places," Rosie remarks, furrowing her brow.

"Yes, that does sound like a rumor that would be convenient for them to spread," Holly sighs. "With their close ties to the Dragonfly Court and access to portals and magic, they are the most likely to walk among you. The veil is thinner in the vampire's domain."

"So, they could be…"

"Anywhere," I answer grimly, clenching my jaw.

"Including our world?" Clara asks, and we watch as my sister gives an uncertain nod. We do not seem to be making progress, despite the new information. Not only does it all seem nonsensical, but it is hard to focus on the sound of each voice with the entire group speaking at the same time.

"Is that why she was able to send us a message using her cellular device?" I ask.

"It is likely." Holly nods. "With any hope, she will get use of it again. We could use a little help."

I take a deep breath, trying to keep a hold of myself. I should have been here…

Surely, I would have sensed something—been able to protect her. And yet, whatever it takes to get her back, I will do. Even if it means blood on my claws.

"Surely there is a way into their domain," I press. "We have people—troops, spies, I am sure! Someone to deploy to give us a way in."

"Spies, yes." Holly shrugs. "Whispers will return to us even from the shadows, but as much as I would like to rush in with my blade, we must take a much-dreaded path…"

"Which is?" I ask, crossing my arms. What could be worse than waiting around and doing nothing?

"Diplomacy." She groans. "I like it as little as you."

"We must get her back!" I argue, speaking more sharply than I should, but the importance is not up for debate.

"But we *must* not start a war," Ruby adds gently. Her hand rests on my shoulder, as she draws in a deep breath; subconsciously, I begin to mirror her, breathing steadily, fighting to find calm in this madness.

"Conflict with the vampires means conflict with the Dragonfly Court. They are closely allied with the Bumbles and their forces are not to be trifled with. Eclipsica has been at peace for centuries. We cannot let this incident throw off the balance," Ruby explains it as a mother would to a child, patient and slow. It is clear that history is being watered down. Whether it is for the sake of myself or the humans, I could not say.

But in this moment, I cannot think of the cost—only that I would set the world ablaze to feel her spark—to ensure her safety.

Still, we follow Holly's plan and wait. The ticking clocks around us make every passing minute feel like agony.

"Brother—a moment please," Holly says, guiding me away from the rest of our group. The parlor feels dry and stuffy, and I am eager for fresh air. It does little good, and I find myself disappointed when the cold does not soothe me.

"What is it?" I ask, walking to the edge of the balcony.

"There was ... something odd that happened at the party." Holly bites her bottom lip, and the calm of her strategic planning has waned. Now, she only looks like a worried little sister. It is unsettling. "It is no matter. I'm sure it was my imagination."

Odd? Anything could be helpful, even if it does not seem like it in the moment.

"Tell me," I demand. "If there is anything that could be helpful, I must know."

She huffs, pacing the length of the balcony.

"No, no, it was—" She turns on her heel. "My assumptions have gotten us into trouble in the past."

"Sister," I beg. "*Please.*"

Her blue eyes grow wide. In portraits, she bears a great resemblance to our grandmother, with the round features of the Butterfly Court, but the furrow in her brow is like looking in a mirror. "Fine, yes, well, there was something odd between Heather and Oak..."

"*Odd?*" I echo.

"I do not know how else to explain it."

"They are friends," I answer plainly, I have never sensed anything strange between them. The pair joke readily, and often get lost talking about creative projects but never in a way that has felt romantic.

"It was if they had something to hide," Holly says, before throwing her hands up in surrender. "I am not trying to cause problems, brother, I promise you. It is just … at the party before Heather disappeared, they were whispering in a way that seemed to be causing Heather discomfort." She presses her lips together tightly. "I overheard something about stealing her away. I had assumed it was a joke. I cannot believe Oak would have anything to do with this, but he did leave before she disappeared. What if—"

My body moves of its own volition, hurtling back into the room until Oak's pale neck is encased in my hands.

"*Whoa!*"

"*Moth!*"

"*What are you—*"

"What do you know?" I growl, raising up his thin body until his legs kick in the air.

"I don't—" He gasps, his hands reaching for mine to try to escape my grasp, but it is a pointless struggle.

Lies. He is lying. Though my memories of the past may be hazy, I can see it in the way he won't meet my eyes. Sprout paws at my shin in protest. I roll my eyes, loosening my grip from his thin neck to the fabric of his collar. Sprout whines, suggesting the change is not merciful enough.

"You know, I used to enjoy when you did this–" Oak grunts, as he begins to shift, his mouth contorting into something pointed and beaklike. "In this context, it is considerably less pleasant."

"Not the time, Oak!" Ruby scolds, placing a hand on her hips.

Mother breezes into the room. "Children please—if you're going to battle, at least adorn your armor and go to the training grounds." She taps her foot impatiently as if worried we'll knock over a vase if we do not take the rough housing outside, but this is not a game.

"Not until he tells me what he knows," I snarl through gritted teeth, loosening my grip on his throat. I suddenly feel more like a rebellious teenager than a grown man searching for his fiancé.

"Right, right. Yes!" Oak takes a deep breath, his human features returning. "Fine! I will. Just put me down!"

"If you hurt her——"

"No, no, no… it's nothing like that. I was just hoping she would change her mind."

"About *what*?"

"The studio! Gods, Moth, will you put me down?" he asks, kicking his legs. Sprout huffs, pawing at my leg once more. Finally, I relent, placing Oak back down onto his feet. *Is that what this is all about?*

"Studio?" Holly asks, tilting her head. Rosie and Clara share the same puzzled expression.

"A business venture … *here* in Eclipsica," I huff. Oak rubs his neck. "I am sorry."

"What did you think—that *I* had something to do with this?" he snaps, looking like I've hurt him more emotionally than physically.

I run my fingers through my hair, unsure how to respond. My desperation is making me reckless, but I cannot let suspicion—or rumors—turn me against my friends…

"I do not know where she has been taken, but I do know we will find her," Oak says seriously. He grins, his fangs on full display. "Besides, I've always wanted to storm a castle. It's all deliciously dramatic."

I roll my eyes. It did not take long for him to get back to his old self.

"What? It is not every day we get to rescue a princess. Though, I suppose her title would not have become official until—"

"Enough!" I growl, pinching the bridge of my nose "Can you offer something more useful than this commentary?"

"*Indeed.* I'll take my leave and comb the taverns for gossip," Oak says. "Perhaps Widow can assist; people tend to have loose lips during gown fittings…"

"A good thought." Ruby sighs. "We can make a list of nobles while Widow works her magic. Goodness, it is already nearly sunrise. Moth…" She bites her lip, a dramatic sigh leaving her lips. "There is something I need from you."

Something I can do to help? I stand at attention and nod.

"Someone needs to get Pepper. They've been promoted to lead advisor while you've been away." Ruby seems a little frantic, and I am happy to offer my assistance.

Mother nods. "Yes, yes! Pepper's expertise will be needed. Get them for us, won't you?"

First, get Pepper. That is an achievable goal. Mother and Ruby smile at each other in a shared moment I do not understand. I offer a shallow bow, turning to leave the room. My body, responding to orders, seems to have a mind of its own. With hurried steps I leave the castle, Sprout following every step of the way.

Pepper has let their hair grow long. It hangs in dozens of braids down their back. Their youngest, Dot, haphazardly adorns the braids with ribbons and flora I suppose must have been gathered from the garden.

"Do you have an appointment?" they ask, blinking their eyes. Pepper looks amused but tired, a beacon of patience; considering that I have been fighting the urge to tear directionless into the sky, it is something I could learn from.

"Heather is missing," I say, surprised at the hollowness in my voice. Pepper tenses, shooting me a look, then glances toward Dot whose tiny hands have not stopped dutifully adding leaves to the braids. From the state of the two of them, still dressed in their night clothes, I imagine it has been an early morning.

"Did you look behind the tree? That's Decy's favorite spot," Dot chirps, and I freeze, realizing I will have to use my words carefully.

"December is quite good at hide and seek." I nod. "I will have to search there."

Before I can say another word, Dot has grabbed my hand.

"Okay, Baba you're all done," she announces, patting Pepper's shoulder to urge them to move. "Uncle Moth's turn." With her meager strength, the child pushes me into the now empty seat.

I open my mouth to protest—there are things to do, orders to give and…

"I take it the queen has sent for me."

"She has."

"Ruby has remained at the castle. Something about her knowledge of the nobility."

"Mommy knows lots of people!" Dot chirps, yanking a handful of my hair. "Decy! Lace! Hornet! July Belle! Uncle Moth is here to play!"

"I—" I begin to protest, but Pepper will need to take their leave, and the children cannot be left alone. I frown, before nodding. My job was to summon Pepper; I had not realized I would also be babysitting.

"Just keep them entertained for a little while… and no flying in the house."

"No fair!" December shouts. In record time, she has flown down the hallway and hovers in the air just above my head. She clutches a handful of ribbons her sister has passed up to her.

In the distance, the sun peeks above the trees, and within mere moments, four more fae children barrel down the steps. I am met with an arsenal of bows and adornments at the hands of Dot, December, and Hornet, while Lace and July Belle focus on giving Sprout a "matching look." I force my lips into a reassuring smile when the weight of the situation feels too heavy. I am sure I look quite the spectacle and Heather would adore it…

She has always been good with them, though she says I am a natural. I cannot pretend I have not noticed the glint in my flame's eyes the few times we've visited, as if getting a glimpse into a possible future. With a smile, I look at the tiny faeries and their artful chaos. Heather was convinced Pepper had over ten children, not understanding that each time we'd seen them they'd simply been playing with friends. Still, five is nothing to underestimate—especially when they are suddenly wielding glitter.

7.

Heather

I **NEVER THOUGHT OF MYSELF AS A DAMSEL.**
Hell, my whole life, I've chased the shadow of my mother; independent, brave, someone who doesn't need anyone to survive. But this is the second time I've been kidnapped in a two-year period and my *#bossbabe* mentality is fading with every second I spend in this room. Something about the way the walls curve makes me feel exposed. Even at my peak, when I was under the brightest flash of cameras, I always craved the cozy corners of my home. With Moth, it's like having a shadow to rest in wherever I go.

But here, this corner-less room lacks safety and all I want is to be home.

My ability to transform is more of a faulty party trick if nothing else, and it's not like I can do much. My nails get a little longer, sure, but I can't shift like Moth or fight with swords like Holly. That attempt was laughable, and something I don't want to repeat anytime soon.

To get out of this, I'm going to have to think outside the box.

He can't have me, but King Magnus wouldn't have done all this if he wasn't pathetically lonely. That might be something I can work with. Right now, the only weapon in this room that I know how to wield is my cellphone—and it's dead. I don't suppose I'm going to find a charger under the random swords and books. God, *so many books*. There are instruments too, some I don't even know the names for.

The more I look around, the more this tower reminds me of the spare room of someone who goes to the craft store once a month to pick up a new hobby after abandoning the old ones. Or, perhaps, the last person who was in this tower had a lot of time to kill. I cringe at the thought that I might be the next hobby he's decided to add to his cart. Pacing, I slip my hand into my pocket.

Despite my stubbornness, I bathed and changed into one of the gowns waiting in the closet for me. It's a silky blush color with dramatic flowy sleeves and a nipped waist. It's not as ornate as anything worn in the Moth Court but undeniably beautiful. Also, it shockingly has pockets, which is a perfect place for me to keep the tiny Mothman keychain I'd been using as a phone charm. I even tied a purple ribbon from the centerpieces to the keyring to try to make it more festive. I run the pad of my thumb across it as I pace the room. It's silly—I knew it when I impulse bought it in Point Pleasant, and I know it now—but it offers comfort.

I wonder if, by now, he knows I'm missing.

The sharp sound of the lock unbolting makes me jolt, and when Magnus steps inside I curse myself for stepping away from him. I wish I could say I'm not afraid of him, but I'm tired of lying to myself. The last time I was kidnapped, I almost died, and the parallels to this situation are not lost on me. I was nice to Chris—too nice. Sometimes I think I might have led him on, but that's beside the point. He thought he was saving me and so does Magnus.

The vampire king holds a golden tray with two goblets and one plate. My stomach practically lunges forward, growling and demanding sustenance after a night of sugary drinks and desserts. To this, Magnus smiles, setting the tray down on the small table near the door.

"It seems my presence is not entirely unwanted." He smirks. God, I hate my stomach for drawing attention to how freaking hungry I am.

I wonder if Magnus knows that humans eat three times a day—and snacks are appreciated.

"I'm surprised it's not stale bread and water," I mumble, crossing my arms. I push the plate away despite the angry, hollow feeling in my stomach. He can't be trusted, even if this is all a misunderstanding. For all I know, it's been seasoned with a love potion and one bite will be my doom.

"My sweet, we both know you can't have bread. I *have* done my research," Magnus says, easing into one of the chairs. He gestures for me to take a seat opposite him. "The staff have been briefed on your medical conditions and dietary restrictions. Your medication will be restocked as soon as what is in your purse runs out." His purple eyes flick up to meet mine, molten and wanting something I'm unwilling to give.

Gratification.

"You bring it with you always, don't you?" He rises, pacing the room with long strides, keeping his eyes trained on me. "For fear of being stuck on the wrong side of the portal with no way of getting a refill…"

How does he know that?

"It seems you've thought of everything to equip my personal prison with," I seethe. He … stalked me? I don't know if it was simple gossip or if he's been following me, but I am totally, completely creeped out right now.

People talk.

He said as much when I first arrived. Given my former job, I'm aware you need to be careful. Drama can start with the smallest comment, the littlest glance, but whatever this is? It's so far beyond that. This dude has been straight up stalking me.

"You're not a prisoner." He frowns. Sensing that his nearness is creating the wrong kind of tension, he takes a few steps away from me.

"Oh!" I shout with mock enthusiasm, walking toward the door. Throwing it open, I note that while I can see a large staircase, it ripples like I'm looking through glass. "Great, let me just head back home then. Since you're not keeping me here in a windowless cell or anything."

Curiously, I tap at the doorway and sure enough it's as firm as stone. I couldn't leave even if I wanted to.

"Seriously?" I say crossing my arms.

"I could not have you leaving before learning my merits." Magnus's eyes meet mine, and I wish I could tell what he was thinking. "But I assure you it is not windowless." He crosses the room and yanks open the locked window—the one with the big wooden bar on it—open with ease. Huh. I guess it was less of a bar and more of a latch—like a hurricane shutter or something.

"This thing has always been sticky," he says casually. Wind blows into the space, cool and fresh, but I keep focused on the opening. When it comes to windows, it's a big one. Sure, I might be underestimating the width of my hips, but I'm pretty sure I could easily fit through it, and best of all it doesn't look like there's any magic around it.

I could bide my time and win his trust, sure, but yeeting myself out the window? Yeah, that feels like a better plan I lunge for it but am easily blocked.

"Wait!" Magnus says, reaching for my hand. He falls short, the whisper of his fingers gliding over my palm without the resolve to take hold. "You may not find the others in the shadows as kind as I am…"

The what?

"I don't find you particularly kind. I think I'll take my chances."

But his tall body blocks the window. There's a nervousness to him that is *strange* in a way I can't put my finger on. Why does he seem so jittery?

"Please—" he begs. "I need you to stay here—for your own safety."

Huh.

I get that the faerie realm has dangers I don't understand—heck, I don't even know what being "in the shadows" means. Besides, the space I can see beyond his body seems cloaked in mist. Totally not ominous at all.

However, there's something else going on here, *something* he's not telling me. Whatever it is makes his cheeks flush pink and his eyes dart nervously toward the window. Magnus regrets opening it. My question is… *why?*

I push past him to get a better look. *Wow.* When he called it "the shadows," he wasn't kidding. The sky is dark, with a fog that obscures any details of where we are. The forest is looming and *dead*. Then my eyes fall onto a short vampire woman walking into the castle on a dark stone path--carrying a floral centerpiece as large as she is.

"What is that for?" I ask, the breath tight in my lungs.

"The court expects a wedding." His face is flushed and pleading, only inches from mine. "*Our* wedding."

A fed-up laugh escapes my lips.

"That's why you won't let me go? You want to save face?" I take another step closer to the window, pushing him away with all my strength. "Hey everyone, guess what?!" I shout down from the tower, but his large hand clamps over my mouth. With a thud, the window shuts.

"Come now, sweet Heather… you will learn that both this domain and I have our charms. Live a life with me surrounded by old tomes and comfort." His tone contains a desperate plea.

"Have you met my husband?" I ask, my cheeks reddening at the slip. Moth and I aren't married yet, but the title feels so right.

"Considering I plan on *being* him by the end of the week, I'd say quite intimately." He leans against the window, barring me from opening it and… God, he's annoying.

"Moth literally reads, makes tea—" *Kisses every inch of my body* "—and scribbles in his notebook all day."

"Huh." He blinks, studying me as if to detect a lie. "From his appearance in Eclipsica last year, I expected him to be into duels and brooding."

"You can't judge someone from one meeting," I say. "Example: when we met, I thought you seemed like an okay guy."

He brightens as if expecting a compliment.

"Now I see you're a total asshole," I say, breaking the long stretch of silence. His smile falters for a moment before the mask slips back into place.

"You don't mean that." He shuffles back toward the door. "Now, please… your body needs sustenance. If my company is too unnerving, eat in my absence. Away from the window, if you please."

"Wait!" I catch his arm. He looks back, face ablaze with the sudden contact. I drop my grasp.

Think, Heather. Think.

There's got to be a way to get yourself out of this.

What is something the human realm has taught you that these faeries and creatures don't have?

"Yes?" He leans in, his fangs on full display as he grins widely, unashamed by his own enthusiasm.

"You want a queen, right?" I begin slowly, the pieces of possibly the silliest suggestion snapping together in my head. "What if I told you there was a different way to go about it than kidnapping unsuspecting women?"

"I want *you*," he says.

"No—you don't, not really." I scramble to figure out my next words. "You want arm candy, someone unknown to your court that they can all be dazzled by."

He leans back, appraising the idea. "Then what do you suggest?"

"We make a deal."

"A deal?" He raises a brow "You want to make a *bargain* with me?"

I nod. It's a formal way to say it, but yeah, if he'll hear me out, I'm sure this is going to work.

"What if I told you there's a way you can meet someone without formally courting them? Someone who will know nothing about this whole situation?" I ask, gesturing between us.

"I'm listening." And he is—his eyes are trained on me like a snake looking at a field mouse. He hangs on every word, ready to pounce depending on my answer.

"I will find you someone else—someone who isn't from your court or mine—to fall in love with."

"In the time before the wedding," he adds, swallowing hard. "Until then, you will remain in this castle—or close to my side."

"Unless you come to your senses and let me go," I say. "Which is the preferable option, just making that clear."

He nods, suddenly appearing more formal. "If you cannot find me a different bride, you will admit your defeat and become mine."

I hesitate. As confident as I am in the harebrained plan that's beginning to form, there's no way I'd actually marry this guy. But, if I get access to my phone, I can contact Moth—and what's the harm in one little empty promise? Especially if it gains me time.

I extend my hand, and he looks … wary. As if he's knows this is all a trap.

"You are certain of this?" he asks just before his hand meets mine. He's planning on keeping me here until I agree to marry him regardless, right? At least this will give me an edge.

"Absolutely," I say, and that's all it takes for his hand to cup mine in a firm shake.

"Then the bargain is struck," he says. At those words, my chest feels just as tangled as a necklace found at the bottom of a purse. "Now, tell me, what is your brilliant plan?"

I meet the predator's gaze, moving across the room to grab my cellphone from the place it's been hidden behind my pillow. "I'm going to need a charger."

8.

Moth

BY THE TIME RUBY RETURNS TO HER home, my worries are hidden deep under piles of dress-up gowns, wooden swords, and a tin tea set with an unimaginable number of stuffed toys centered around it.

I served them a lunch of sandwiches and fruit, and now the oldest are off reading stories, while the three youngest faeries are asleep, using Sprout as a pillow. I dare say this is the most content he's looked all day. And I'll admit that, in the time I've spent chasing after the five children, I have barely had a moment to consider my own problems.

"Seems like you have things under control here," Ruby whispers from the doorway as she slides inside, shrugging off a bag filled with groceries that appear to be from the market. I smirk; apparently, she had been in no rush to return.

I nod, the gesture curt, but all I can manage. Now that it is quiet, worry tangles in my chest like a scream that I am unable to release.

"Have you made any progress?" I ask, clearing my throat.

"A list of contacts. A map of the realm. We are trying," she says warily.

"While I sit and do nothing."

She flicks one of the many braids on my head.

"I do not know… you seem awfully busy." She casts an eye toward the children. "Many things can be said about me, but I have experience in dealing with tantrums."

"You—" I blink as the realization of why Ruby and Mother had exchanged those looks hits me. "You put me in some kind of … time out?"

"You *did* try to strangle Oak."

"…I thought. I do not know what I thought." I shake my head. "Perhaps I know nothing else than how to be a monster."

"Now, I don't believe that for a second." Her slender arm wraps around my waist, guiding me away from the kitchen. "You believed Oak had something to do with Heather's disappearance. It is not unheard of—in either world—to be betrayed by someone close to us. You, my friend—" We are in the entryway of the house, standing in front of a large mirror. "—are a protector, not a monster. Why else would I trust you to watch my most precious treasures?"

"To make sure I am too exhausted to fight?" I ask, and Ruby throws her head back with laughter. We both peer around the corner to see if the sound woke the children. My heart warms at the sight of their wings fluttering as they sleep.

Ruby was my betrothed for years. It is a strange thing to know without fully remembering. If things had been different, could this have been our life? Perhaps, but I doubt I could have ever made her this happy. Not because of a fault in myself—or in *us*—but truly because there is only one person I was made for.

In this house, when I hear the laughter and feel its warmth, I think of a future with my flame at the center.

"Tell me, was it the right distraction… sending you here?" Ruby asks, a look on her face that suggests she already knows the answer. "You seem more at ease."

I nod. It was hard to live in anything but the moment with the five little faeries causing both joy and chaos around me.

"Thank you. I know stepping in to look after them was not an easy task. We all have roles and expertise we can lend. Like Oak, I am a terrible gossip, and I hope that anything I provided to the queen and Holly can help."

"You are more than a gossip," I assure her, admiring the home she and Pepper have created.

"And you are more than sharp teeth and claws." She smiles. Given my decades spent among the mortals, it is easy to forget that. I have been called a harbinger of death, and death itself, in both realms. But strength can be used to help just as easily as it can hurt…

I must keep my wits about me or risk further mothering from both Ruby and Mother.

"How did you know this … change of scenery would work?"

"If it hadn't, I would have had to resort to bribery." She circles back to the kitchen island, the golden light casting a warm glow across her deep brown skin. She unwraps a parcel of cookies and reveals a jug of what looks like apple juice. "Everyone feels better after a snack."

Waiting.

It goes against every instinct in my body.

Heather is strong. She is resourceful with an arsenal of cutting words and charm. She is far braver than she gives herself credit for.

Heather will be fine.

Won't she?

It has been less than a day, and yet it feels like it's been days since I last heard her laugh.

She can navigate this. We will find our way back to each other. We always have. We always will. Still, the thought of her facing these challenges on her own haunts me.

Holly seems … less aggravated than before; the blades have been sharpened and the soldiers have their orders. She stares up at the portrait of us as children. The cold eyes of our father stare back. Oak must finish the modernized version of our family portrait soon. Having just been surrounded by Ruby and Pepper's children only hours ago casts a chill across my skin.

I was a child, just like those sweet faeries, undoubtably with the same toothy grin and laughter. But, as I stare up at that old painting, the small boy I once was stares back at me. How could anyone—much less a father, have raised his claws to someone so … *small?*

When the ghosts from my past become too loud, Heather banishes them with a simple touch of her hand, and when that is not enough, she is quick to hand me a pen, encouraging me to work out my feelings through fiction.

But the portrait is not the only thing that disturbs me. It is that the humans seem to be the only ones as distressed as I.

"It's a shame. I grew to really enjoy Heather," Holly murmurs as she calmly takes a seat next to Clara.

I straighten. Why is she speaking in past-tense?

"She's not … dead." Clara straightens. "Wait, right?"

"No, she is not *dead*," I hiss. "Why are you speaking so strangely, as if you did not declare we would see her safely only hours ago?"

"I was just thinking…" Holly trails off, her eyes still on the painting. "You have been absent from our world for decades and may not remember that this is how a great many of our love stories start. Father whisked away Mother after only sharing one dance." She taps her feet for a moment, as if unsure whether to stay or go. "I say this with the utmost respect, but it is possible that this will change things. Such a grand gesture will surely not go unappreciated by even the most devoted. Right, Mother?"

My heart drops.

If she thinks that is *romance*, we have more to worry about than her murderous streak.

My little sister knows how Father stole our mother away like a thief in the night. She has heard songs detailing their romance and tragedy—a sweeping love story indeed. But clearly, she has not been privy to the other details.

Mother pales, her limbs shake like a leaf rattled by a storm. With unwavering elegance, she sweeps her hand in the air, dismissing her attendants.

"Everyone, please." Pepper bows formally to me before addressing the rest of the group. "The royal family requests privacy as we navigate this difficult situation." And with the grace of a lead advisor, they lead everyone away from the room, whispering reassuring words to our human friends.

"Come, I'm sure the children would love to meet a pair of humans," they say with laughter to their voice. And just like that, the humans are ushered away, and we are alone.

Mother paces the length of the room, wringing her hands. It is unusual to see her looking fazed, much less nervous. But her eyes are far away and her forehead furrows as she walks and walks. Finally, she faces us.

"There is a part of the story I neglected to tell you children." Her voice is strong despite the way her hands shake. Mother eyes me before giving a small nod. "Though I expect Moth already knows. I don't imagine Heather is the type to keep a secret from you."

I wonder if she is about to confess father's murder to us. It is information I have obtained only because, as Mother suspected, Heather told me the first moment she could.

Mother touches the line of her fabric-covered wings, always draped in silk and lace, giving them the illusion of being larger than their true size. The color and shape is a mystery to me; even as a child she never showed them to me. She fiddles with something on the back of her dress.

"What part is that, Mother?" Holly asks, her eyes widening.

Ribbons rustle, and with a thud, her wings fall at her feet. I gasp. Such an integral part of her appearance now lies like discarded laundry on the floor.

"The part where I tried to escape." She turns to reveal two long scars peeking out of the bottom of her low-backed gown, and the air in my lungs rushes out.

My flame. What horrors could you be enduring while we are apart?

Heather

THIS IS TORTURE. LITERAL TORTURE! I shut my eyes tight; the world pulses red around me until I take a deep breath.

"You have got this all wrong!" I shout, flicking away countless photos of Magnus from the camera app. Who knew setting up a dating profile for a king from another realm would be this difficult?

"I beg your pardon?" Magnus stiffens beside me, snatching the phone from my hands. He swipes through all of the photos I've taken.

As pretty as he is, he photographs with the vulnerability of a stone. Each photo is the same, save for a subtle movement of his chin. And there's something else too—Magnus is too perfect. He is the definition of uncanny valley, everything is too symmetrical, with teeth too straight and gleaming, and skin free of pores and any sign of aging.

It's like he has three beauty filters layered on top of each other, and the end result is a face so perfect it's … unsettling.

"I look exquisite," he huffs. "What is the problem?"

"Okay, you know what…" I shake my head. "We can work on some candids later. For now, just fill out your bio. Likes, dislikes, and stuff."

"Understood. Though, I don't know why we are bothering." He holds the phone close to his face as he types out what appears to be a novel about himself. "It seems pointless to search for a match when the most beautiful woman in the realms is seated across from me."

"Considering I *don't love you*, I think you maybe want to up your standards." I reach out my hand and he hands my phone back to me. My eyes flick over the bio and he's *got* to be kidding.

"What is wrong with what I've written?" he says, and I have to assume the disappointment is showing on my face.

"Vampire King looking for queen to share his throne." I groan, tossing the phone behind me. Magnus effortlessly catches it and tosses it back to me. Considering it's a piece of equipment I desperately need, I decide against any further rounds of catch. He hasn't given me one moment unsupervised with the device, but he's got to let his guard down sooner or later. As soon as he does, this is my ticket to getting a hold of someone back home.

"It took you *that long* to type this?" I gasp. Crossing my arms, I wonder if I can slip the phone into my pocket unnoticed. We're never going to get anywhere if he isn't going to take this seriously. "Plus, don't you want someone who doesn't care about your social standing—to fall in love with the real you and whatnot?"

"I typed out what will give us the fastest results," he says thoughtfully. "Would you like me to add an astrological sign, my sweet? It seems everyone has something along the lines of that… or a random assortment of letters. What is an INFJ?"

"You're clearly a Scorpio and *so* not an INFJ," I grumble, reaching for the keychain that's still safely hidden in my pocket to ground myself.

"As far as an astrological sign, I am a Leo, and the other, perhaps we'll leave it out." That also … checks out. We still need more than that to work with. How am I supposed to explain this to him?

"Okay, look…" I decide to just lay it all out. "With editing apps and makeup, a pretty face isn't enough to attract a real connection. You're way too stiff and there's nothing conversational here."

"You just called me pretty." His smile is absolutely devious, and I wish he would stop getting distracted.

"For someone else," I counter as damage control. "You need to write a bio that makes someone else want to strike up a conversation with you! This whole thing is giving AI bot energy, and no, I'm not going to explain what that means."

He scoffs and snatches the phone back, scrolling while looking long and hard at the screen.

"We will make conversation when we meet. You don't expect me to court someone using this device, do you?" He gapes, blinking his purple eyes as he stares into the light of the screen.

"That is exactly what you do—and literally *no one* is going to take this profile seriously!" I try to explain. "First off, most mortals don't think vampires exist. You need to dive deep!"

"Then fix it!" he grumbles. My phone is thrown back to me like a baseball—and I'm not a good catch. "Or marry me; you already know I would prefer the latter."

"Literally … you're impossible." I snatch the phone off the floor and thank the stars for my industrial-strength protective case. I walk toward the window—which I cannot squeeze out of no matter how hard I try *and I have.*

It's unsettling to be in a new place every day. Instead of the forest, we're surrounded by a lake as black as the night. The lack of sun makes it impossible to figure out how much time has passed. Working on Magnus's profile has felt like an eternity in the worst possible way.

"Okay, okay, let's slow this down. What kind of stuff do you *actually* like?"

He freezes.

"Well, I am accomplished in all things from instrumentation to language, if you would care for a demonstration I can certainly…"

Not an answer.

"But what do you like *doing*?" I squint at the screen. "Because I'm not seeing anything of value written here, and if you could work in a few details—"

"If I list out everything I am skilled in, we will run out of space." I frown at the obvious unauthenticity. "Surely a human will be impressed by the idea of royalty?"

"Okay, sure, but you're more than your job title," I try to explain. "It's like someone saying, *'I'm a lawyer looking for a girlfriend.'* It doesn't tell you anything about them except for how they make money."

"But people love money," he says, and this time it's not sly, it's earnest. The sad fact is I don't know him well enough to assure him it's not the most appealing thing about him.

"You are *so* missing the point." I groan.

"Then explain it better." He pouts, crossing his arms. *I wouldn't need to explain it if you would just listen.*

"Okay, Mr. Moody," I exhale, pinching the bridge of my nose in the same way Moth and his family do when they're frustrated, "let's move past what your skills are, and just tell me about your favorite things."

"Why would anyone—"

"Just list them off," I grumble, wondering if a second attempt at running him through with a sword would be worth it. "Favorite food?"

"I am a *vampire.*"

"Right, right, okay, we'll avoid that." I roll my eyes. "Color?"

"Would it be too bold to say the color of your eyes?" he croons, and I close them tightly at the slimy pickup line.

"What color are they?" I ask.

Silence.

"Green." His response is confident and so very—

"*Wrong.*" I frown, still keeping my eyes shut tight.

"Blue."

"*Seriously?*"

"Heather," he pleads, clearly getting sick of this little exercise.

"Favorite color … *now.*"

"Red."

Cliché, but again, I'll take it.

"Perhaps we leave it all blank." He shakes his head. "We could be exact opposites and still find kinship."

"It's something real…"

"Which means?"

"It's a start." I shrug. Honestly, the thing I hadn't considered when I suggested this hare-brained plan is that

I've always been terrible at online dating—and dating in general. Most people I met were at industry events or set up by friends. I've swiped left more than I've swiped right. Even still, if Magnus will just listen to me, he'll have a date in no time, and I'll be free.

"I do not see why personal details will matter," he says. "Keep it as is."

"But it says nothing about you!" I shout. We are going in circles—*again.*

"I assure you, it says all anyone will care about," he repeats. Ugh, I *so* do not have it in me to give this guy a pep talk. Still, I look into his eerie purple eyes and try to level with him, careful not to pull any punches.

"Okay, clearly that's not true. You've reminded me *how* many times, and I literally do not care, and neither will any other mortal. This is a casual reminder that they don't know vampires *exist.*"

"That is … a point I had not considered." He slumps down next to me. "What do humans take interest in?"

"Okay." I brighten at his ability to finally listen. "First you need to let people really get to know you."

"But that is so much work," he whines, falling back into his chair. "How will I find a bride before the wedding?"

"And kidnapping me has been smooth sailing?!" I stumble back, my vision spotted with red for a moment. Taking a deep breath, I try to center myself. I've got this. *I've got this.* Just stay calm, Heather.

"Point taken," he grumbles. "But, for the record, I thought it was a—"

"Rescue. I know, I know!" I throw my hands in the air. "How would it have gone if it was?"

A blush covers his face before he gulps heavily and averts his eyes.

"You would have thrown yourself into my arms, and my bed, happily reunited with the man you fell in love with at first sight." A cocky grin plays across his too-perfect face, without so much as a glimpse of the nerves he'd had seconds ago. He speaks flatly as if reading them off a script.

"I wouldn't have just wanted a physical connection; I would have wanted something emotional too," I admit. It's not like I've never had a hookup before, but he pales in comparison to the monster waiting for me at home.

"I can, I *will* be patient. I understand all of this has been unexpected," he says softly, "And, for the record, I am sorry. In truth, before you suggested this deal, I had a mind to let you go, even if it did mean I'd be a laughingstock."

Like hell he did. I know his type; he's just trying to find the right pretty words so that I'll let my guard down.

"Focus on the dating profile," I urge and damn. *I miss Moth.*

Magnus's smile falters, and for a moment. our eyes meet. I'm struck by the undeniable sadness that's heavy in the hues of purple. How long has it been since he's let someone in?

"So, it won't do to charm them with my title and good looks?" he asks, a little more pouty than I would have expected.

"It might get you some dates but, if you really want to date mortals, wait—" I groan. "Have you ever actually dated anyone?"

"Are you suggesting—"

"That your romance experience is mostly flings and grand balls?" I interrupt. "Am I wrong?"

"You're not." He hums thoughtfully tapping his chin "And you think I won't perform well?"

"I think we're starting at square one."

"That settles it," he says, grabbing my hand and pulling me toward the doorway. To my surprise, when he's the one who pushes on the door, it ripples like it's laced in portal magic. *Interesting.*

"Where are we going?" I shout, digging my heels into the ground.

"To practice."

I have to admit, I've been curious about the Dragonfly Court ever since Holly mentioned the giant lily pads. I have to say, it doesn't disappoint.

Magnus and I sit atop an oversized lily pad in the center of a lake; weeping willows stretch across the sky, their mossy ribbons creating curtains that divide the lake into different rooms. We are in the middle, where we can be seen by all; when the server flies to our table with menus in-hand, I can feel all eyeballs turn to us.

When he said he was going to take us out to dinner, I thought it would get me closer to the mortal realm, but this… this is more of a fairytale setting than Queen Plume's castle.

"It is one of my favorites," Magnus says, lounging on the lily pad as though it's a picnic blanket. "I think you might like it too."

"Oh, shut up." Of course I do. I mean, there are tea lights and flowers floating in the water.

While my present company leaves little to be desired, it's fucking magnificent.

"So, this is your court then…"

"My mother's," he corrects me, and there's a break in his usually masked expression. So… half dragonfly fae, half vampire?

"But you don't have wings," I say. With the way he raises his eyebrow, I realize that was probably rude. But no, I'm not going to worry about being a jerk to the guy who kidnapped me—whether or not it was accidental.

"So, you shift too?" I ask.

"What do you mean *too?*"

"Well, in the mortal realm, I just kinda suck my wings into my shoulder blades, I guess?" I say. "I'm sure you guessed I was human before."

"I had my suspicions there was something … *unique* about you." He laughs. "It was one of the many reasons I was drawn to your presence. You see, most people of the winged courts have a distinct pattern and a name to go along with it."

I frown. It's something I've noticed and googled after our first trip to Eclipsica. The bugs that exist in my world have patterns shockingly close to the wings that adorn the backs of my new family and friends—even Moth. Though, I think his pattern is softer than the Death's-head hawk-moth, *prettier too*. Still, it's made me wonder if the patterns represent the magic that bleeds across the realms.

"I thought you'd be a Luna by the coloring," he muses studying me with an intensity that makes me shiver. "But the pattern is unlike anything I've ever seen."

"And your wings are similar?" I press. He averts his amethyst eyes.

"You hide your wings by shifting in the mortal realm—the antennae too, I assume?" he asks with a deep frown, fully intending on ignoring my question. "Why not use a glamour?"

"Oh, it sucks, but it's better than having invisible wings bumping into people all the time. Plus, everyone knows; when I'm home, I don't shift at all anymore."

Almost everyone. A pang of guilt shoots through me as I think of my mom.

I wonder what Moth is telling her while everyone sorts this out. I should have said something. It's not like we never talk; things between mom and I have been healthier than ever, except for the whole me lying about being part faerie thing. Okay, not *lying* but also not telling.

"Are you shifting right now?" I ask, craning my neck to take another look at his back.

"No," he says, his face falling into a grimace. I fight the urge to trace the space just above his shoulder to see if he has wings hidden there.

I could badger him more; getting him to hate me with awkward conversation could be an interesting strategy. With a sigh, I look out at the clear water, watching the dragonfly faeries fly so low they nearly skim the water, delivering orders to creatures of all shapes and sizes.

Despite our recent argument, Magnus seems more relaxed, lounging upon the lily pad with his fingers trailing through the water. The moonlight shines upon his hair, making the red almost appear purple.

"Can I take your picture?" I ask. "Just stay like you are."

He brightens, slipping the phone out of his pocket and handing it over. As soon as I train the lens on him, that stiffness returns.

"Just try to be natural, like you were a second ago," I coach. "Tense and untense your jaw, wiggle your arms a little—okay, now relax, relax—*perfect!*"

I snap his picture; it's not quite as at ease as how he appeared gazing into the water before, but it's definitely an improvement.

"Where did you learn to do that?" he asks, still transfixed by the water. "I understand mortal technology is different, but the idea of capturing someone in their natural state is so…"

"Novel?" I offer, borrowing the words Oak used in his pitch to me. "Just wait until you see an instant camera."

"If you are the one who will show me, I cannot wait."

I roll my eyes at the shameless flirtation. I suppose the attempt shouldn't surprise me since we are supposed to be on a date.

The server comes, interrupting our conversation and Magnus's attention. The phone is still in my hand. I palm it, slipping the device into my bodice, hoping he won't notice. Considering his eyes have a dreamy far away expression, I think I've gotten away with it.

While I bide my time, I turn my attention to the food that arrives—some kind of fish pastry with caviar on top for him, and what looks like pink roasted vegetables wrapped in bright green leaves for me.

"This is perfect," he says, raising a cup of tea to his lips. For him maybe—but I'm on a date with the wrong person, and the phone pinches my ribs from its hiding spot urging me to find the right moment to escape.

"But temporary, you know that, right?" I say, knowing I should play nice, but unwilling to let his contentment slide.

"That seems to be common sentiment," he huffs. I'm so sick of this. He knows I don't want this, and the fact that he doesn't care makes my skin feel tight—like I'm physically about to burst out of it. But it's the word "common" that gets me.

"*Oh?*" I say. "Because if there happens to be someone else who thinks this is a terrible idea, I'd love to meet them."

He doesn't bother to give me an answer as he picks at his food. Interesting. I had assumed his meals would consist of golden goblets of blood, but it's surprisingly human to see him take a bite of something that looks like it belongs in a seaside bakery.

"If you have questions, there is no need to hold back," he says, poking at the food on his plate. "Your former lover may not have been a good guide when it comes to this realm. I promise to fill in any gaps he neglected."

That sounds … *weirdly sexual*. Magnus must hear it too because his face reddens. He coughs as if to rid himself of any further awkwardness.

"With *information*, if that was not clear." His inflection is clumsy and unmeasured.

"I'm fine, thanks." Regardless, I'm bursting with just about a million questions that are still unanswered.

"Come now—humor me with your curiosity."

"You can eat real food," I say, a statement not a question, that's actively being answered with every bite he takes.

"As long as all other needs are met, I function as anyone else." He shrugs. "I suppose the faerie part enjoys it more than others of my kind. You will not see a lavish spread of cakes and sandwiches in my domain. Here, though…" He smiles down at the plates set before us, and I have to admit it all looks stunning.

"What's up with all the stuff in the tower?" I ask. "No offense, but it looks less like a prison and more like a storage unit."

"Have you considered it is neither?" His violet eyes level with mine. "More of a refuge for someone who spent … much of his youth alone."

"So, it was your hangout?" I laugh. I guess normal kids have treehouses, maybe this is the fantasy version of that. "How many of the instruments can you actually play?"

"All of them," he says, and I think he might be telling the truth. "Though I have a fondness for the Hurdy Gurdy."

Despite myself, I laugh.

"What?" He balks. "It is the large stringed one, with the crank, and flowers engraved on the—*why* are you still laughing?"

Yet another reason not to trust Magnus. He's definitely making this up to mess with me, because even in a world of faeries, vampires, and monsters, I don't think an instrument called a Hurdy Gurdy exists.

"Is there a court you prefer?" I ask, pressing on and ignoring what looks like embarrassment on his face.

"It is hard to say." He gestures vaguely to the serene setting around us. "The Dragonfly Court feels like walking through my childhood. This castle, however, is my future— one I have imagined with you."

"No, you've been imagining someone me-shaped. We don't even know each other," I say, waving the thought away with my hand. I pick up something that looks vaguely like a carrot and dunk it into a pink dipping sauce. While I can't quite place the flavor, it reminds me enough of a veggie platter to keep eating.

"Then let me get to know you," he says, placing his hand on top of mine. His skin is cool and soft … and not Moth's.

"Let me ask you this—" I free my hand and point at him with another one of the veggie sticks. "Who is your dream girl, and *do not*—I repeat, do not—say me."

His lips curve into a smile.

"Then I fear I must remain silent," he says. We might as well be on a reality dating show with how thick he's laying it on.

"I don't think you could if you tried."

"See! That is what I like about you: the bite to your humor is so refreshing." He tilts his head back with a laugh, and it makes me wonder…

"Magnus, if you want to find a girl to be mean to you, there are whole apps dedicated to that. I can—"

"*No, no*—that will not be necessary."

"Okay, but that's an angle I can work with—and this whole possessive bad boy with a heart of gold thing isn't working," I groan. "Believe me, I would know; I've got one at home."

"I beg your pardon!"

"It's not your vibe."

"And what is my *vibe*?"

"That's what I'm trying to figure out!" I snap, waving the carrot-like stick back and forth. By the way his brow furrows, I wonder if he even knows himself. How long has this man been performing and who is it for?

"You're never going to be my type." I shrug. "You'll be someone's, but we won't know who until we—" An involuntary yawn escapes me and Magnus gapes.

"Am I boring you?"

"I haven't exactly been sleeping well," I reply, longing for the foamy lattes of the mortal realm or the strong black tea back in the Moth Court.

Without hesitation, Magnus signals the server over and orders something I don't quite catch the name of. They flutter away, returning with a glass serving tray that mirrors the leafy shape of the lily pad we're seated upon. On the tray balance two cups filled with light pink liquid that seems to glitter in the light.

"Try it," he says, gesturing for me to pick up the small mug as he does the same. "It is a specialty in this region of the Dragonfly Court."

"It *is* pretty," I admit, raising the pink glittery cup to my lips. If he wanted to poison me, he would have already done so by now. The drink is fragrant with the scent of almonds and beetroot, and it's honestly delicious. It reminds me of one of my favorite tea blends back home, though this one is much more sparkly. I don't know if it's waking me up, but it is nice. Once I'm home, I might ask Holly if she can find a sachet of it to add to my tea collection.

"What can I do to ensure you are well-rested?" he asks, and it's weird how worried about it he seems.

"You could let me go."

"A new bed perhaps," he offers, steamrolling over the suggestion.

"It's not the bed," I huff.

"Ah." His eyes glint. "Not used to sleeping alone then? That's not what I heard…"

"What?" I snap. Considering I'm usually sandwiched between Moth and Sprout, things are the opposite of alone. I can't imagine what he's talking about.

"Last time you were in Eclipsica with your brooding fiancé, the servants reported he left you every evening…"

Oh.

Is that what it looked like to the rest of the world?

"That's *so* not what was going on." I'm not about to explain to this guy that Moth was processing a shit ton of emotions in the form of writing a novel. Magnus might have me locked in a tower, but he doesn't get to know Moth. Not his kindness, not his vulnerability.

Let him think the love of my life will storm the castle and rip his throat out at any moment.

"I could stay with you until you fall asleep," Magnus offers, and I nearly spit my drink.

"Absolutely not."

"I'm not suggesting anything improper. I could sit at your bedside and read to you if that would—"

"That's Moth's job," I snap, feeling my nails curl into claws. I gulp down the rest of the tea, trying to let the feeling build. I wonder if my transformation would scare Magnus enough so that he'd let me go. But not here… not when there are so many witnesses.

"Heather?"

"There's a bathroom around here somewhere, right?"

"Around the corner, behind the giant green stalks to the left." He points toward the main building that resembles an open-air cafe suspended above the water. "I can accompany—"

"Magnus," I hiss, "you want me to feel like I'm not a prisoner, right?"

"More than anything."

"Then let me walk to the bathroom by myself."

He sighs, so lonely and pathetic.

My claws retract, and I let out a frustrated sigh.

"I suppose there's little harm."

The phone hidden in my bodice pinches as I flutter upward, moving toward the reeds Magnus had pointed out. Part of me worried it would literally be just a spot to pee in the lagoon, but, sure enough, there's a building here.

Waiting until I'm tucked around the corner, I retrieve the cellphone, moving around until it finds a signal.

Without hesitation, I dial every number I can think of, hoping to hear his voice.

10.

Moth

"There are pieces of truth mixed in with what you might know," Mother begins. "I was indeed *kidnapped,* but not from one of the other courts or a noble household of this world. When I was young, it was not uncommon for faeries to steal away into the mortal realm. Mostly for some trickery—whether cruel or comical, it depended on the level of boredom."

"But you met father at a ball…" Holly says quizzically. She has clearly already decided this is all some kind of shared delusion. Mother stares off as if entranced by memories, walking toward the window, the steps of a waltz echo on her heels.

"In a place called London, my sisters and I were so excited to spend the social season among the affluent. We were well-off, but Mother raised us in an estate in the countryside, among flowers and trees. She always said the city was no place for a child—but women in need of a suitor? Well, that was when things changed. I was terrified but excited all the same. I loved the simplicity of the life I lived, but had little desire to climb the social ladder. All the same, I wanted to find love—real love. Meanwhile, your father craved amusement while visiting the mortal realm. He was bored of bars and brothels, and his beauty was enough for him to gain entrance to high society. Our eyes met, and he decided that I would be his queen."

A mortal…

This is a part of the story I hadn't anticipated. Perhaps this is why she took Heather under her costumed-wings.

Mother turns to both of us before I can begin to process this new information.

"Each day, he visited with a flower—a promise. As he saw it, I had no choice but to love him, to need him. But I was not a Cinderella looking for an escape from the life I had before. I was loved by friends, family, and my sisters. Affection for your father did not happen overnight." She blows out a sigh, tracing her fingers over the ornate floral carvings of the portal.

"I do not understand," Holly says. "You two always made it sound like something from a storybook."

Mother blinks in response, nodding sharply and sucking in her breath before regaining the posture of a queen. How long has she been forced to push down her feelings to serve her people? She does not answer Holly—instead her eyes lock on mine.

"You are familiar with the gifts you share with your father?" Mother asks, and though it is a question, it feels more like an accusation.

"Yes." A dark feeling echoes through my chest as I wonder how this will relate to Mother's tragedy. There is knowing in her eyes that once her secrets are told they cannot be unlearned and with that comes hesitation. Her thin hand grips Holly's before she speaks again.

"The first time I tried to flee, I was mended by him using those powers." Her voice is hollow and further away with every passing moment. "I awoke in darkness, reborn as one of the Moth Court, just like our dear Heather."

"First attempt?" Holly pales. "You tried to escape more than once?" My sister studies Mother, who only nods in response.

"You had wings?" she asks, though it sounds more like an accusation than a question. Mother gives another stiff nod in response. "You mean to tell us Father gave you the power of flight and then—"

Mother clears her throat.

"He said the wings were damaged beyond repair. I imagine they were in a state similar to yours, my son, when Heather cured your wounds the mortal way." Mother stares at me and there is a deep knowing, that if someone like my flame had been there to tend to her, things may have turned out differently.

"So, they could have—he could have—" Holly stares at Mother, her crystal blue eyes glassy.

"What was given was taken." She clasps her hands together. "We can assume they could have been patched the mortal way—but there is no way to know. There is a reason you never see me *flutter* around the gardens. If it helps, I had them for so little, I do not miss the feeling."

The scars on her back have not healed well, as if the focus had been on removing them quickly rather than care. I have no doubt this act was done in anger. From what I can remember of the man it seems, to borrow a term from my flame, "very on brand for him." If Mother had not killed my father, I would do it myself. I can bear the pain he caused me—but to do this to his wife…

"And you have not used the aid of magic?" I ask. It is a surprise considering she is the one who provided the glamour I now use in the mortal realm.

"Ah." She moves across her chambers, picking up a necklace. When she puts it on, it gives the same effect as her costume, but her fingers pass through the wings, breaking the illusion with a sparkle. "It is not effective by itself. At a large function, I wear both."

"This is not what you told Heather," I say, reeling with these new pieces of information. Heather only learned that Mother was kidnapped…

"*Heather* knows of this?" Holly whirls, more hurt than angry. Mother only nods, letting silence fill the room for a moment. To my surprise, my sister does not press the issue.

"She learned more than most, my love. When you are queen, you must take time to determine who you can trust. After Atlas's betrayal, I have been more careful." She runs the pad of her thumb across Holly's cheek.

I grit my teeth at the memories that have resurfaced about Uncle Atlas. There are days I fear I conspired with him. I was too young to rule and needed a way out. Perhaps I asked him to send me to the mortal realm—perhaps my memories were taken to ease my guilt. The facts remain; I was cast out by my uncle, and as a result he took the throne until his disappearance.

"You two really were friends with Uncle Atlas," Holly says, drawing in a deep breath.

"The best of friends." She smiles bitterly. "He was my confidant. While I dealt with your father's tantrums, Atlas would be a shoulder to lean on, always keen to distract me or listen to my stories. He was fascinated with the mortal realm—"

"He was the one who gave you the portal then?" Holly concludes. "I always wondered."

"Yes." Mother's smile is bitter. "We found it poetic to put it in the tower, a gateway to freedom in the place that was my cell."

"Why not just go back?" I ask. Given she had access to a portal, the most logical solution would be to return to the mortal realm.

"Ah, by the time he gifted me the portal, my family was long gone. And I had you—nothing to return to and every reason to stay." She smiles brightly, holding both mine and Holly's hands, losing the formality in her tone and her tactical smile—her words are true.

"This whole time, you… you never told us," Holly says, unable to hide the hurt in her voice.

"No, no I did not." She frowns. "I planned to—perhaps one day when the time was right. Before you took the throne or, well, I'm not sure."

"When could it ever be right to learn something like this?" Holly gasps, shaking her head. "Oh, Mother—" she cries, and I brace myself for an angry outburst.

Instead, she wraps herself in Mother's arms, squeezing her tight. "I am so sorry—"

"Do not worry, my darling. I received two treasures worth any hardship," she says, opening her arms so that I can join their embrace.

"And she poisoned him," I add.

"Moth!" Mother scolds me as if I'm a child who said his first swear word. And something in her tone puts a smile on my face. After all that we've been through—secrets revealed, names changed, and being a world away—she is still my *mother*. The patient face that shines through my lost memories.

"Oh, good." Holly sighs, squeezing the two of us tighter. "It will take time to unravel the idea I have of him, but knowing there was an act of retribution helps."

"The truth is complicated," Mother admits. "There were moments it was… he was—" She shakes her head and sighs. "But perhaps that was just my mind helping me to survive. One thing is certain: we *must* rescue Heather."

Holly pales, nodding vigorously.

"I am sorry for my outburst, brother," she says. "I should not have made light of the situation. Perhaps I thought that this would all be less maddening if she had planned it herself. I have seen how much love she has for you. Even King Magnus would not be able to change that."

"It is forgiven."

"Are we very much like Father?" Holly asks, her gaze tipping up at the family portrait.

I freeze in anticipation of a less than favorable answer. The resemblance between us is so striking that I cannot look for long.

"No, my darlings, you are uniquely you." Mother squeezes us tighter before straightening. She taps my chin with the tip of her claw. "Wonderfully and uniquely you." Sprout nudges my leg, pushing the three of us together to share one more embrace. I gather myself with a deep breath.

"And you are lovely," she whispers, and tears I did not realize had formed roll down my cheek.

It has been hours since the conversation with Mother, yet as my claws trace along the keys of the old piano, I hear not a sound. My thoughts turn from fear, to rage, to sorrow in the absence of my Heather. Then there is the fury of learning the truth of what happened between my Mother and Father. The same fate will not befall the darling sweet human who put color back into my world of black and grey.

The gall this vampire king has to take her for a bride… Furious, I focus on the keys of the piano. It is my first time alone since all of this begun, and I allow my mind to wander.

When was the last time we were here together? It was months after our first time in Eclipsica. Mother had decided to throw another one of her parties. I was going to decline, but Heather had just bought a new dress and was eager to show it off for more than just myself and Sprout.

I couldn't blame her. The color was a sky blue in a soft tulle, and when she danced, the dress seemed to dance with her, swaying with the curves of her body. The sight of her smile alone was enough to make me ache.

But *that dress*…

The cyan-sheened fabric hung off her shoulders like cascading water…

Even in my memory, the decadence of her presence tempts me. As my fingers stroke the keys, I let my thoughts drift away. Though my hands still move across the keys, I think not of the notes, only of her.

The lilac scented breeze blew through the room, ruffling her hair, sending tiny strands across her face. Positioning herself so that her body leaned back against mine, I wrapped my arms and wings around her like a cocoon.

"Do you know how to play any other instruments?" my flame asked, a coy smile on her pink-tinted lips that begged to be tasted.

"No, I do not believe I learned anything beyond this."

"You're full of secrets."

"The only things I am keeping from you are the things I myself cannot recall."

"What a good excuse to live in the moment then, huh?" she said, her hand sliding across my thigh. "Let's make some new memories."

With a few skillful movements of her hands, the laces of my trousers loosened. I would be glad to be free of the whole garment, but I waited patiently while my flame dropped down to her knees, leaving me to straddle the piano bench.

"Keep playing," she ordered with a wicked smile. And I obeyed. How could I not when her voice sounded like honey? Though, the music of her moans would be the sweetest I could think of.

Turning my attention to the sheet music, I focused on the notes, the movement of her hands, then her lips across my skin. Pleasure and tension built up in my body, and though my fingers stroked the keys, the real conductor was beneath the piano. My flame slid her hand between my——

I slam my hands down on the keys as footsteps ring out behind me.

"Hey bud, how you holding up?" Rosie asks, the scent of herbal tea heavy in the air, suggesting she has brought me a cup. I cannot bare it; closing my eyes tight, I continue to play. I meant to return the mortals—I truly did. But the pair insisted on staying, and I cannot lie: they have been an unexpected comfort.

The cup is placed on the ledge, and whether it is the honey in her voice or the drink that brings me back to the moment, I do not know.

"Do not patronize me." I groan. Anything could have happened in a day's time. Two years ago, I watched Heather's life fade by way of a bullet that was meant for me in only a few moment's time. "How long have you all been here?"

"Long enough," Rosie replies. I am sure that they could see the haze in my eyes and blush to my cheeks while I sat here, lamenting. I decide it might be best to not ask anyone leading questions. It seems Holly, Oak, and Rosie have all been watching me daydream at the piano, and I am thankful that the memories that surfaced did not last long enough for me to do anything foolish…

But my desire for Heather is unfathomable, and the fear that I will not be there in time to save her is too horrible to conceive of. My patience has bounds and waiting for diplomacy has pushed them too far.

I'll never forget the horror of seeing the light in her eyes flicker into something unfocused and far away. I acted before it was too late, and now my flame shares the power and burden of my abilities. But *what if I had not found her in time?*

A world without my flame is too miserable to bear.

"I'm not trying to downplay this. It's just… I don't know, Holly told us this kind of thing happens here. It seems like everyone is making progress. Plus, there's no way Heather would marry anyone else."

"I have been corrected," Holly grumbles. With a glance toward to the family portrait, she grimaces before tossing one of her knives directly into the painted face of our father. "The danger is not to be underestimated."

"Oookay." Rosie nods. "Then remind me exactly why we aren't all *freaking out?*" There's an edge to her voice now.

"I think we covered that earlier, didn't we?" Oak says casually, wringing his neck from his place on the chaise lounge "What stage of grief are we currently in—shall I get my armor?"

I shoot him an undeserved glare. I should never have lashed out at him.

"Heather has helped me overcome my monsters," I say quietly. "It pains me that whatever she is facing, she is doing it alone."

"Moth…" Rosie's voice is quiet. The scent of the tea she brought wafts toward me from its place on the ledge of the piano. I draw in a deep breath, muttering an apology to her and Oak.

As far as my memory serves, I have never been good at friendship. Still, I accept her drink and kindness. The text Heather sent said she was safe.

I will just have to trust in that until we have a lead. If we are to rescue Heather, we will need some sort of plan that involves more than rumor-hunting and diplomacy. My wings itch to fly straight for where she's hidden, and my claws tremble to feel King Magnus's flesh turned to ribbons in my grasp. My hands slam down on the keys before pushing myself away from the piano bench.

"Let's just try to *distract* ourselves then, hm? It worked for you earlier at Ruby and Pepper's house, right?" Rosie says slowly. "Oh, I know! How is the manuscript going?"

My writing? I let my jaw go slack. That is what she wishes to talk about now?

"It is of no concern at this moment," I say, burying my head in my hands. Before all of this, the writing had been an easy distraction when I could not sleep at night. I did not anticipate finishing it. Or to "query" it for publication, something Heather has encouraged me to try. She says it's "too good to sit in a notebook forever," and I will not deny there is some part of me that craves to be known—not a blurry photograph but in a way I can choose.

"Oh, come now, brother! Indulge us if not a little bit," Holly says encouragingly. I suppose I can update them, though it may not be the uplifting shift in conversation the group is hoping for.

"It has gone well," I begin. "The e-mail replies however have noted I have archaic prose and a genre-crossing plot." The rejections are of no consequence, though I do not think it is good conversation.

"It will find a home," Rosie says, though the deep frown on her usually smiley face is … telling.

"Of that I have no doubt."

"It's not like a creative to be so sure of themselves," she says, nervously tucking a strand of red hair behind her ear.

"I found one—a home I mean." I shrug, closing my eyes and thinking of the life I built with Heather. "So there is hope for it yet. Even if it does not amount to publication, it is an outlet. My former life in Eclipsica is hazy at best."

Holly's frown deepens; I should have chosen my words more carefully. My absence has caused her hardship, and I do not mean to add more melancholy to the already dreary mood.

"That must be hard," my mortal friend says gently. I nod, unwilling to say anything further.

The hardest part is being unable to design a new creative thought with a memory. Some days, I think I might have wanted to be sent to the mortal realm to avoid being king.

Other days, I'm sure I was trapped there.

Mostly, I do not think any of it matters.

So, I use it for fodder for a fictional man who carries my flaws through a world of romance I try not to mirror too closely to my own. Though writing out a very detailed scene involving the murder of a vampire king may be a cathartic solution in the midst of all this waiting.

"Rosie, you should have let him keep playing the piano." Oak sighs.

"This is … worse somehow," Holly agrees.

Ah—I am back to pacing. For how long now, I am not sure.

"Heather has been stolen away," I growl through gritted fangs. "How is it you expect me to act?"

"By leaping into action and ripping someone's throat out, *naturally*…" Oak says, rubbing his neck. I open my mouth to apologize once more, but Oak waves my bad behavior away. "We all understand. The wait has been torturous and, in our own ways, we will fight at your side."

"Patience has never been a virtue I have readily had in my possession," I say, lowering myself into one of the gilded parlor chairs.

"We just need to figure out which throat to rip out," Rosie says, giving me a hearty pat on the shoulder. The cheerful tone combined with the grotesque suggestion would be comical if this all wasn't so dire.

I knew being with me would have dangers. I worried about my form, my claws, and the bite of my fangs. What I did not give enough thought to was the worlds around us, and the way the people in them would pull us apart.

I had hoped the human hunter would have been our first and only foe.

Clara sprints into the room, waving her hands in a wild motion.

"The lavatory is down the hal—" Oak begins, but she shoves him out of the way. I realize she's holding a small glowing object in her hands.

Her cellphone. It's shoved into my palm before I can fully grasp Clara's sudden reappearance. She had wandered out for fresh air, and her phone must have found a signal. Still, *this* is unexpected. It must be her. There is no other reason why Clara would have burst into the room in such a way, but as I raise the device to my ear, doubt creeps through me.

"My flame?" It is a question, a prayer, and a plea all in one.

"Moth!!" Heather's voice wraps around me with the comfort of a cloak. Despite languishing by the piano for hours, no sound has ever sounded more like music to my ears than my name from her lips.

"Heather!" I stand so quickly the chair topples. "Where are you—I will—"

"It's okay! I'm okay! Well. you know, as okay as I can be," Her voice crackles. "I'm biding my time. Basically, there was a … *misunderstanding.*"

"A what?"

What kind of misunderstanding would cause a kidnapping?

"Okay, so like, basically… Magnus thought I agreed to marry him at that ball we went to in Eclipsica. It's a whole big thing, and now I'm trying to set him up with someone else. So, we made his dating profiles earlier, and I was able to get my phone back and—"

"You are … trying to do *what?*" My claws extend, and I swallow hard in an attempt to keep myself calm. *Magnus.*

She's calling him by his first name.

"Babe, he's literally *so* pathetic," she whines. I can almost see the way her full lips pout at the words. How I wish I could kiss her, to feel the softness of her skin, and stop this ridiculous plan all at one. But she continues all the same.

"He's fixated on me because I helped him at the ball when he was cornered by those awful butterfly twins."

"My flame, you have been … making an internet online dating profile for your kidnapper?"

"Well, when you say it like that, it sounds silly," she says, and I can just picture her crossing her arms.

She cannot be serious.

"Have you considered, my flame, that that is, in fact, *because* it is silly?" I ask, using my free hand to rub my temple.

"No?" she says after a long pause, and despite myself, I chuckle. She is ridiculous, but she is mine. "Yes! Yes, okay? But all the portals are warded and… look! I finally got my phone and I've been—are you *laughing* right now?"

I should not be, but I cannot help it.

The tension I was feeling breaks as a deep chuckle rumbles through me. She is alright, and the sound of her voice swirls around me like smoke lingering on skin after sitting by a bonfire.

"You are alright," I breathe. When I close my eyes, I picture the way she looks with her dark eyes creased in a smile.

"I'm alright," she whispers back, and I imagine her leaning forward so that our foreheads touch, soft and tender.

"You are alright," I repeat, shaking my head. "Here I have been worried about finding you in mortal peril, and you are playing matchmaker for your captor."

"Yes, babe, I'm safe, I'm okay, and I think this plan is going to—"

"Fail," I cut her off. The cold graveness of the situation brings me back to the moment.

"What? No!" She gasps. "I finally got the pictures we need for his profile. At this point, all we need to do is get swiping, and we should have Magnus enthralled with someone else by the end of the day. If he takes his dates to this gorgeous place, any mortal will be dazzled—if they can accept the whole vampire—"

"It is destined to fail," I interrupt again, trying to mind my tone. She clearly believes this will work, but there is a fatal flaw she's not considering.

"Wait, why? I am being so detailed and—"

"Because there is no one who would not fall in love with you. You cannot sway him, Heather. Besides, I do not believe his affections to be true."

"But there's only one person I could ever love." She sighs and I wish I could hold her in my arms. "I'm trying to get back to you. If Holly knows how to disenchant portals, put her on the phone. Magnus seems like the only one that can use them, and right now, we're in the Dragonfly Court. I only have a few minutes before he comes looking for me."

"Where in the Dragonfly Court?" I ask, too afraid to hit the speaker button for risk of accidentally ending the call.

"Um, a restaurant. I don't know what it's called. It's on the water with lily pads as the tables. Does that ring any bells?"

Of course it does not.

"Holly will know of it, I am sure," I exhale, trying to be optimistic. "Do not think your plan will convince me to stop looking."

"Oh my God, please don't." She sighs. "Just because I don't think Magnus is dangerous doesn't mean I don't want to get home, just don't—"

"Heather," I warn, "do not ask me to spare the man who took you from me."

"I mean, rough him up, obviously. You have my full permission to avenge, just don't full-on murder him." She laughs, and I wish I could see her smile, though none of this seems amusing.

"He will not be able to recognize his own face."

"That might be a fate worse than death, to be honest."

"Good. I love you, my foolish little flame…"

"I love yo——"

I barely hear her response before Holly springs up, taking the phone from my hands. It drags me back to the present moment. I am in a room filled with a people who have been staring, listening to my every word.

"Heather! This is important. You are helping him with a … task?" Holly presses her mouth against the phone's speaker.

"Did you make any promises? Agreements?" she shouts, but the call has ended, and our chance to get further details with it.

Do we have enough breadcrumbs to lead us back to her location? Across from me, the room has erupted into conversations about diplomacy and negotiation. I overhear words like territories and allies. I barely register them, holding myself back from lunging into the nearest portal alone. Without Heather here as the angel on my shoulder, my restraint doesn't last long.

"Where are you going?" Holly asks.

Without realizing it, my body has transformed. With large strides, I walk toward the doorway. "To get her back."

All the thoughts. All the thoughts swirling around—with the noises of so many people talking at once—has me on edge. She would know what to do. Yet, she is the only one who isn't here. After being alone for so long, it is a funny feeling. I have only half of a heart; she holds the other. I will not rest again until I see her smile.

"Then let's go—together," Rosie says, straightening up.

"Together?" I quirk an eyebrow, while Oak and Holly shoot disapproving looks at her. The humans may have insisted on staying here and helping, but besides the needed mortal support, I do not see the value of placing them in danger.

"No, no, I will go—as will Pepper, who will serve as Mother's right hand," Holly says, leaving little room for argument. "*You*, Clara, and Oak will all remain at the castle."

Rosie crosses her arms, not willing to back down so easily.

"Heather's one of our best friends. The first time she was kidnapped, I couldn't do anything. I didn't even know what was happening…"

"And what will you do if there is a fight?" Holly pipes up. "Bake cookies at our attacker."

"Hey!" Clara says. "*I'm* the one who bakes cookies. Rosie is also good at baking, and honestly everything, but she's also—"

Rosie plucks a knife from Holly's arsenal and tosses it. It plunges into the apple at the very top of a pile in a decorative bowl clear across the room.

"—really good at throwing shit." Clara chuckles, sidling up to her wife and giving her a kiss. "Have fun, hon."

11.

Heather

"*I love you, my foolish little flame.*" Moth's prickly voice seething through the phone has sent warmth back into my cold body. I can just picture the way his jaw clenched, his red eyes flaring. God, I want him so bad. Even if he can't understand my *genius* attempt to bide time.

I wish I'd been able to hear the rest of Holly's questions. Why would it matter if I agreed to help Magnus? All we said were words; it's not like I signed a contract.

I try and try to get the call to go through again before conceding and slipping the phone into my bodice. It digs into my ribs, but thankfully, with the way the dress is made, it won't be spotted. I turn the corner, examining the restaurant. The trouble with it being open air is the exits are both everywhere and nowhere. Plan or no plan, Moth is coming for me. But if there's a town nearby, I might be able to find someone to help in the meantime. This meal will end soon, and Magnus will want to take me back to his castle…

I spot Magnus—still at our floating picnic on the water. More food has arrived in my absence, and he stares off as if lost in thought. Considering I have a contraband phone hidden in my bodice, I'm glad to have a moment where his full attention is on something other than me.

Moth is right. This is a silly plan, and this is my chance to change it.

My wings stretch out before I can talk myself out of it, and I fly skimming over the water until the restaurant is a blur behind me.

"Heather!" Magnus shouts behind me. I cringe, sparing a glance over my shoulder. Despite being part of the Dragonfly Court, he doesn't sprout wings and chase me. Instead, he stalks across the marshy ground, hopping from lily pad to lily pad until there's nowhere left for him to go.

But it's strange. Something inside me aches, similar to when you leave home and can't remember if you left your hair straightener plugged in. *Why do I feel like I'm supposed to go back?*

Shaking my head as if to dislodge the thoughts, I push forward, ignoring the sensation until it's a dull hum at the edge of my thoughts. My wings take me past over-grown reeds and flowers. Directionless, I dart forward. The water turns crystal clear, reminding me of the way Queen Plume's portal ripples. The magic that's used is supposed to stem from this court, right? Maybe the solution is even closer than I thought. I find myself distracted by the way the water shines and glimmers. It's so hypnotic that I can barely tear my eyes away, which is unfortunate because my wings have clipped a low hanging reed and now I'm crashing into it.

Splash!

I close my eyes tight, anticipating the shaky feeling of portal travel—but it's just water, and now, not only am I directionless, but both me and my cellphone are soaked.

Great.

"No, no, no, no," I hiss through gritted teeth, kicking my legs to stay afloat until I get to one of the oversized lily pads to hang on.

Searching the area, I notice a dock a little off in the distance—along with some kind of building beyond it. Maybe I can find someone to help me or, at least, lay low for a moment. I swim toward it, the feeling that I didn't unplug a major appliance returning the farther I get, not that I have long to focus on it.

Something shifts in the water in front of me. Bubbles rise to the surface, and I yelp, unsure of what kind of predator could be lurking under the surface. Before I moved out of Orlando, we had gators which were bad enough.

I have a feeling anything living here wouldn't hesitate to eat me. The top of a head rises until a pair of yellow eyes stare into my soul.

"Ah!" I scream, swimming faster toward the dock. I flutter in a vain attempt to fly, but my wings are soaked and heavy. Oh my god, whatever is coming for me is fast. I don't think I can outswim it.

The creature glides like a gator cruising toward its prey before it rises from the water. I reach the deck's ladder, but barely have a chance to climb it before a man covered in green scales rises from the water.

"Well, howdy." And damn, I don't know what I was expecting, but it certainly wasn't a southern accent. The man's frog-like yellow eyes blink at me, one eye at a time.

"Oh, um… hi." I pull myself onto the dock, slumping over as I catch my breath. The fish man follows suit, and I wonder if maybe this place is his.

"In a mighty hurry, are you?"

"You could say that." I shake the water from my wings. "You don't happen to know how to get to the mortal realm, do you—*ah!*" A sudden pang shoots through me, and I fall with a thud onto the dock. I gasp, realizing it's not a hair straighter or an oven I want to turn back for… it's Magnus.

Gross.

I hate him. I think. I mean—I don't want to fall into his arms or kiss him, but there's a need that spreads through me. I feel like if I don't get back to him, my chest is going to explode. It is as though he is the sole key to my survival.

"Okay, hang on here, ma'am. Take a deep breath—you hurt?" the fish man asks. While I don't know how I feel about being called "ma'am," I can't exactly object to the help. My heart races as he bends low to get a look at me. I manage to take a breath, scanning my surroundings to try to ground myself.

I breathe in the scent of salt water, touch the rough wood below me, and note how beautiful my surroundings are. A cottage sits at the edge of the dock. I think it might look like the kind of place mermaids live, but I don't have the luxury of marveling at it, not when it still feels like my chest is going to explode.

"One breath at a time," the fish man urges, his southern twang oddly comforting. He splays out his webbed hand as if to reassure me that he means no harm. "Just stay right here," he orders before running inside. He returns with a glass of water.

"Gil, pleasure to meet you, ma'am." He hands me the glass, and despite how shaky I feel, I manage to drink.

"Heather—you don't need to call me 'ma'am.'" *Please.*

I'm not sure if it's the water, or the breathing, but the pressure on my chest lightens. It's not exactly the ideal time for an anxiety attack, but then again, it never is.

"There a reason why you look like you're running for your life out here?" Gil studies me as if to check for damage.

"Well, I kinda… you wouldn't happen to have a portal to the Moth Court, would you?" I sigh. "Or the mortal realm?"

"Depends on how long you can hold your breath." He looks down into the deep crystalline water—and oh my god, yeah. Unless magic is involved, I don't think I can swim down to the bottom of the ocean. "You in some kind of trouble, miss?"

"I'm literally being chased by a vampire who is holding me captive right now… so, yes."

"A *vampire*—" He draws in a deep breath. "Okay, Heather, is it? Don't you worry. I happen to know exactly who to get to help—"

Suddenly, we're eclipsed by a shadow, and when I spin around, Magnus lands on the dock with a thud. The lingering ache in my chest dissipates.

I take a step behind Gil, choosing to trust a stranger over the vampire who has been keeping me against my will. The pain on Magnus's face makes me almost feel guilty.

"By the four sisters…" Gil groans. Even with his fishlike appearance, I can recognize the posture of someone who is fed up. "Please tell me *that* isn't the vampire."

"That's him." I groan, not having time to linger on who "the four sisters" are and what swamp monsters might worship. I cower *behind* Gil. Not out of fear; I know Magnus won't hurt me, but I want to do everything I can to create distance between the two of us.

"Why would you act so recklessly? You know the terms of our deal!" Magnus pants. He looks worn out and more than a little disheveled. "Do you not value your life?"

Okay, that's a tad dramatic, even for him.

"What are you talking about?" I ask, the ache in my chest finally lifting now that he's back and—*oh my God.* "You're the reason my chest felt like it was going to explode?"

"Magnus, you didn't!" Gil shouts. No title. Just pure exasperation. Gil blinks a few times before turning his attention to me. "You're *that* Heather?"

Great, they know each other. As if that isn't bad enough, the vampire king's pining has gone beyond daydreams and a wedding playlist. It's all a reminder that while I might be counting down to my wedding in the mortal realm, Magnus has sent out his own invitations—and my name is written under *bride* in both.

"Is she not perfect?" Magnus says softly, and while he still looks unbelievably angry, his gaze softens when his eyes find mine. *Gross.*

"And y'all in some sort of … agreement?" Gil questions, holding up his hand to keep Magnus quiet. You know what? I think I like him. My thoughts get caught on this whole idea of an agreement. Holly asked almost the same thing before our phone call cut out. That can't be coincidental.

"It's not like I've signed any paperwork…" I say, searching through the threads of the conversations Magnus and I have had in the little time we've spent together for anything damning.

"Heather, my sweet, this is the second time I have stated my very clear intentions." Magnus pulls at the strands of his red hair. "You have agreed to stay in my castle or at my side—and find me a suitable match by the end of the week."

"I didn't think it was binding!" My eyes go wide while I look between the two men. This has to be a mistake.

"How?" Gil and Magnus reply in unison.

"I'm kind of new here, okay!?" I clutch at my chest. I've been around faeries for a year now, and while Moth doesn't remember enough to fill in the gaps, shouldn't someone have warned me about this kind of thing? If a bargain is as easy as a few spoken words and a handshake, we're lucky I didn't get into trouble sooner.

"How do I get out of it?" I ask, panic starting to set in. "Because, full offense: I would rather eat a live cockroach than marry him."

I don't need to look at Magnus to know that he's gaping in horror.

"That should be the easy part," Gil says through his laughter. He turns to the vampire king, "Surely, you'll let her go now that this misunderstanding has been—"

"I won't give up earning her favor just because of a few missteps!" Magnus cuts him off, as determined and stubborn as ever.

"Take. Her. Back!" Gil shouts with the sternness of someone trying to tell their housecat to drop a dead mouse.

"No," Magnus replies, his tone flat and uninterested. "We still have two days, and I intend to win her over by the end of them."

"Magnus!" The fish man's gills flair as he lunges toward the vampire with his yellow claws splayed.

"*What?*" The vampire king narrows his eyes, his teeth bared. "I have been imagining my life with this woman since she agreed to be my bride last season."

I take a step backward. I'm used to Moth's grumpy expressions. It can be fun to make him a little angry from time to time, but Magnus is still a wildcard. I haven't seen the depths of his temper, and I'm not taking my chances.

But it's Gil who has the advantage here. He leaps in the air with unexpected ease, tackling Magnus onto the deck with a resounding *thud.*

In mere moments, the vampire king is flat on his back. Hastily, I search the area for an escape, running down the uneven wooden dock toward the house.

"You can't just kidnap people *you* want to marry!" Gil shouts, just as Magnus floats—literally *floats!*—up, knocking Gil off his feet. My new scaly friend, however, is agile and grabs Magnus by the ankle, his claws sinking into the vampire's flesh. Just like that, Magnus is pulled back down to solid ground and trades blows with Gil on the dock.

"I'm not taking relationship advice from the man who's been pining over some human for over a decade. You know, if *you just*—" A splash cuts off Magnus's words as the two crash into the water. It's deep, but still they fight just as easily as they had on land.

"Do you know how expensive this coat was?" Magnus shouts, reduced to a whining fashion model as opposed to royalty.

"You'll buy a new one!" The swamp monster wrestles him under the water.

"It's vintage!" Magnus shouts when he resurfaces.

In this fight, I'd have my money on him. In the moment, I can't figure out if this is a brotherly spat or he's about to murder my captor. Can vampires even drown? I don't know, but this whole violent scene is making me uneasy.

I don't want to marry the vampire king.

But I don't necessarily want him dead either.

"Okay, okay, okay!" Magnus sputters. "You have made your point."

"So you're taking her home?" Gil asks, seeming to be ready to call it quits.

"Home to my castle, of course," Magnus croons. Yup, not the answer Gil or I wanted. Gil dunks the vampire king back under water.

The two spar with violent splashes, and as much as I would love to keep watching this train wreck of a fight, this is my best chance to escape. But the dock is wet and considering I am the clumsiest person I know, I slip right as I reach Gil's house. The walls look like they're made with sea glass and shells and hurt like hell when my arm scrapes across them. Just like that, the splashing from the scuffle behind me is replaced by eerie silence.

Rising from the water on what I have to assume are glamoured wings, Magnus floats toward me; his eyes flash an unnerving red, as if possessed.

Blood. I gulp—this isn't good. The vampire king stares at where the red drips from my forearm. It wasn't even that big of a scape, but damn, the blood drips pools.

Magnus wouldn't hurt me, *would he?*

Gil has climbed up onto the dock, matching Magnus's stride, and soon, both the men are inches away from me.

"Heather, darling," Magnus purrs. Yeah, no… I do not like the way he's saying my name.

"Nope," Gil says, pushing Magnus back off the dock. "I'll patch her up. You look for a way to redeem yourself."

Magnus bobs up from under the water, fully soaked. I'm thankful that when he opens his eyes, they're the usual purple hue.

"We are in love," Magnus shouts, not bothering to climb out of the water this time. "She just has yet to realize it."

"I can drown him if you want," Gil offers, and I can't help but laugh at how genuine he sounds. "On a day like today, it would be a pleasure."

"As tempting as the offer is, my fiancé has first dibs on ripping his throat out." I shrug.

"I can still hear you!" Magnus shouts, and if I didn't feel so shaken by the way he had zeroed in on me, I might laugh.

"I was hoping that would be the case, you old bat," Gil says in a sing-song as he leads me to his home with the gallantry of a knight.

To say the small stilted house is cozy would be an understatement. There is dark wood paneling, and a collection of paintings that look like they have been lovingly collected from thrift shops. The whole place has a dated feeling with the smooth round lamps in pops of burnt orange. I note the sunny yellow mugs hanging on a rack in the wood paneled kitchen. There's even a shag carpet in the living room, and the furniture looks straight out of the 1970s. But most unexpected of all is the albino alligator comfortably lounging in the middle of the room like a scaly nightmare puppy.

I jump; this is exactly the thing I was trying to avoid.

"That's just Clawrece. She's a good girl—aren't you, baby?" He leans down and says, affectionately scratches under the gator's chin like she's a beloved pet, and she must be by the way her mouth lolls open showcasing a row of sharp teeth. Her long white body lounges on the orange rug in a way that reminds me of a creamsicle. Is this adorable or am I losing my mind?

You know what? Could be both. The one thing I know for sure is today absolutely could not get any weirder.

"Can I get you something to drink? There's water, lemonade, seaweed juice…"

"Seaweed juice?" Okay, maybe it *can* get weirder.

Gil cracks a smile.

"Had to see if you were still paying attention," he drawls with a shake of his head. "Make yourself at home. I'll get the first aid kit."

And within minutes I'm sitting on a swamp monster's couch, having my scraped arm bandaged. Considering what my life is like, honestly this all checks out.

"Have you lived here long?" I ask, breaking the silence that's been surprisingly more comfortable than awkward.

"It was my grandfather's," he says, his voice slightly wistful.

"Oh, I'm sorry."

"No, he's still alive, just moved in down the water a little closer to my folks." He smiles. "It's a tight-knit community around here."

His grandfather. Huh, I wonder if that's who gathered all the vintage decorations. Either way, it's welcoming and quirky in the way it's hodgepodged together.

"So, how exactly do you and my kidnapper know each other?" I ask as he skillfully wraps my arm. Given the whole fae thing, it shouldn't take long to heal, but I'm not exactly eager to get back to the tower. After this little stunt, I'm sure Magnus isn't going to take his eyes off of me.

"Magnus grew up attending most of the big parties at the Dragonfly Court," he says.

"And you?"

"Grew up sneaking into them." His smile echoes the childhood mischief of his past and makes me curious just what kind of trouble he and Magnus got into together when they were kids. The flicker in his yellow eyes is almost gold in the sunlight, and even with his scaly appearance, I can totally see his charm.

"He was always a quiet kid, loved his books and his hobbies. I suppose that's what happens when you spend most of your time alone," Gil says as he wipes down my small wound with something that stings. "I was always able to find enough mischief for both of us. Now, it seems he's finding it all on his own."

"Wait. Isn't he like, thousands of years old?"

"Magnus? Gods no."

"But you called him *old bat*."

"Because he's two years older than me. I can't imagine how insufferable he'll become by the time he's a thousand—though I won't be around to see it. Thank goodness, huh?"

I nod. Moth and I have only briefly gone over the specifics of faerie lifespans and we can stay old and hot forever-ish. Vampires seem like they might be even more invulnerable. But what does that mean for someone like Gil?

"We Gillerians have a lifespan closer to a human's in the peak of health. We make it about one hundred years, sometimes a little older," he offers, seeming to read my mind. Which isn't something I think he can do, but nothing would surprise me at this point.

"So, you're called Gillerians, and your name is Gil?" I ask, hoping it's not rude. Moth is the prince of the Moth Court and while his name is something I picked for him before those memories returned, I'm not one to judge something for being on the nose.

"Full name is Gilbert," he says with a sheepish look. "Family thing. Anyways, one hundred years might not seem like much to a faerie, but I'm more worried about living without my love than dying." He, wistfully looking out the window toward the sparkling water.

"She's in the mortal realm?" I ask. I overheard Magnus making some kind of crack during their fight, but it was hard to figure out the meaning without context.

"Marina," he says through a drawn out sigh. "It's been so long; I'm not sure she'd even remember me."

"What's she like?" I ask, because honestly, I *love* love. From what I've seen of this swamp monster, he deserves happiness.

"She's like—" His lips turn downward, and he shakes his head. "Well, she was brave, kind, *so kind*, never thought twice about my scales or—" He ties off my bandage with a bow before patting my arm lightly. As if to tell me I'm good to go.

"We met as children. I thought she was the most beautiful girl…" He shakes his head, placing his webbed hand on his heart. "I don't know if or when I'll see her again, how we'd feel about each other. But there's some kind of love that'll always be etched right here. She probably wouldn't even recognize me."

"I think you'd be hard for a human to forget."

"Well, then—when I find her, that means I'll have a chance. Even if it's just at friendship."

"Yeah." I smile, flexing my freshly bandaged arm. "I'll be rooting for you."

"And I do appreciate that." His eyes glimmer for a moment. "Now, ask whatever question is hanging on your lips."

"You said something about the four sisters?" I ask. "I've never heard anyone from the Moth Court talking about worship, but they sounded like … goddesses?"

"The faeries don't tend to worship much apart from themselves." He shakes his head. "Magnus included. But it's a tradition we have in the water. The sisters represent each season; there are festivals, mostly an excuse to see family and eat food."

"Those are the best kind of holidays." I smile. "I shouldn't ask, but you said Magnus was alone a lot growing up. Why?" Knowing what Moth's told me of his childhood, just because you're a prince doesn't mean you have an easy road. But Moth had friends like Ruby, Oak—and romantic flings with almost every person I've met here. He may have been lonely, but he wasn't alone—not all the time, at least. Magnus might be a different story.

"That happens when a kid feels like a spectacle everywhere they go," Gil answers with a thoughtful hum. "His parents split when he was young. Magnus's father was the sort who only wanted perfection, you know? They kept him in lessons—by the time we met, he could perform every formal dance, speak multiple languages, and play any instrument you could think of. He was painfully shy, and surrounded by people who never said 'no.' Which is why he's probably drawn to people like you and me. The personality he's normally showing is just another dance."

"So, he's not usually like this?"

"Not always." Gil rises from the table, walking to a small shelf. He snags a framed photograph. There seems to be a lot of human touches to this place which makes me wonder who they're for and how they got here.

"A photo from one of our celebrations," Gil explains with a wistful smile. "We've spent a lot of time together. He was the one who consoled me when I had my first heartbreak, and I'm the one who's been telling him to just be himself; sometimes, I think he's forgotten how. Things changed when he went to live in his big dark castle. "

"Burn down the spooky dark castle—got it," I say, knowing that isn't the point Gil is trying to make but unable to muster up any more empathy.

"Won't help much. He's become more withdrawn since becoming king." He sets the photo on the table and packs up the first aid kit. "He shows up here when his head gets stuck too far up his ass and I throw him into the water."

"So that…" I point out the window toward the dock. "Was a normal thing?"

"Mmm," he hums thoughtfully. "I'd say you got the special edition show, but we spar like brothers when he needs some sense knocked into him. I've become some kinda unwilling advisor, and I can't say I love it—but I do *love* him like family. Now, make his life hell, Heather."

Wow, was *that* a lot of conflicting messages!

"Why don't I hate him?" I ask. "I keep toeing the line of being mean then helpful. I had this whole silly plan to set him up with someone else, but I should hate him, right? Is this a part of the bargain?"

Gil smiles, shaking his head. "Nope, that's just Magnus." Great, if it was a part of the deal, at least I'd have an excuse. What can I do to make Magnus *want* to let me go?

You'd think me not wanting anything to do with him would be enough. Magnus doesn't feel like he could ever be boyfriend material—for me, at least. In any other time or realm, he would be friendzoned no matter how handsome he is.

Gil and I walk outside together, clearly in cahoots, and Magnus groans at the sight of us.

"You're supposed to be my friend, you know," Magnus grumbles, stalking back toward us like a drowned rat.

"And I'm having second thoughts on that every minute I have to look at you," Gil says. I can't help but laugh.

"Now, are you ready to go?" Magus asks, holding his slimy hand out to me. I stare at it, unwilling to move.

"No." I shake my head. I'm not moving an inch until he breaks this deal—and from the way Gil steps in front of me, I think he agrees.

"I can't in good conscience let you take this lady anywhere," Gil says. The threat, combined with the accent, makes me wonder if he's going to challenge him to a duel at high noon. Which, honestly, I would be totally here for. A southern gentlemen, why couldn't I be trying to set *this* guy up?

Even with the scales, I think he'd be an easier sell than Magnus. Whoever Marina is, I hope they find each other again.

"So, what? You'll keep us here until I agree to break our contract? No, I don't think so," Magnus replies. He's standing tall and clearly not going to back down here.

"Do you want me calling the whole family in on this? You think you can outswim us all?"

"No," Magnus says, and there's a panic on his face that makes my hair stand on end. "But I can fly." It all happens so fast: a gust of air, Gil falling backward, Magnus striking him with a rock in his fist. Oh my God!

I'm sorry? Aren't they supposed to be best friends?

Then I'm in his arms, being launched in the sky with such speed I can't even scream, the wind knocked out of my chest.

I thought I was safe. I thought he wouldn't hurt anyone. But now—

"Stop!" I finally manage to get a hold of my voice. I push at him until he releases me, and I plummet downward before I'm able to catch myself with my own wings. Panic pulls at my chest; will I survive if I try to run again?

"Heather—"

"What the *fuck*?!" I scream, and no—no, he seriously didn't just knock out his best friend in the name of keeping me his captive. "Say the words. Release me from this pact or whatever *right now*!"

"He should not have stood in our way," Magnus says dismissively, his eyes level and angry. Is this who he really is? It's not at all the pathetic lovestruck snake I've painted him as. *This* man is ruthless.

This is the vampire king.

As he hangs in the air before me, light shines through his now exposed wings. They're thin and dragonfly-like, albeit iridescent with the scalloped edges and veins of a bat. He flies well, but they're almost too small for how broad his shoulders are. They remind me of something you'd buy in a pinch before a renaissance faire without checking the dimensions online.

His pupils grow until his irises are barely visible. I wonder how often he lets himself be seen in this shape, and at the same time, I don't care at all.

"The swamp creature has taken worse blows than that," he assures me, tugging at my wrist, but I fly backward, unwilling to let him take me anywhere. "He'll survive."

"You can't make me come with you," I say with all the defiance I can muster, but I am exhausted, and it shows.

"No, but you will follow." His voice is pure venom. "Or do you really want to see how far you can get this time?"

"I hate you." I hope he can tell I mean it.

"Yes." He nods, a hint of the sadness I normally see in him has returned. "But you'll come with me all the same."

12.

Moth

E HAVE REACHED THE DRAGONFLY Court, the scent of her honeycomb soap lingers in the air, promising she will be just around the corner. I ache to feel the softness of her skin against my own...

Heather.

Oh, love of mine: too trusting. Too loving—too sweet. Yet, one taste of her decadence would never be enough. When I find this vampire, it will not do to simply snap his neck. I am going to—

"Moth?" Rosie's voice is quiet.

"What?"

Rosie squeaks in response, and I realize I've half-shifted in flight. My eyes cast a red glow across her face, and I breathe in deeply, trying to collect myself. I cannot.

"You just look like you were about to murder someone."

"I might still," I groan, scanning our surroundings. We have been following the sweet scent of honey and … blood. A chill runs through me knowing it is hers.

Holly's nose wrinkles as her and Pepper speed behind us, confirming I am not the only one who is worried. Heather said this vampire would not hurt her, but what if she was wrong?

My talons scrape against the wood of the dock as we land. Carefully, I deposit Rosie onto the ground. The red-head lets out a shaky breath and a frown pulls at my face. I should not have brought her. But with the way she insisted, I did not have the resolve to refuse.

"I am sorry if I did not put enough care into my flight…" I begin. If my movements have been as frenzied as my thoughts, I fear the human might need time to adjust.

"No, no … I'm fine, it's just that I've never flown before." She lets out a laugh. "I feel like I'm in a fantasy novel."

"Let us hope it is one where the princess is rescued by the end," Holly says. The old wood creaks as she lands on the old wooden dock. "The server who reported seeing Heather fly off said she had come in this direction. Do you suppose she took refuge in that building?"

"The scent of her is everywhere," I answer. There is no doubt my flame lingered here—whether she remains is another story. As we approach, Pepper remains searching the perimeter in hopes to find a lead.

But for now, this house in the middle of the water seems our best lead. We walk forward on the old dock until we reach a small cottage. It is whimsical in the sense it looks like it has been carved from sea glass and shell. Even more striking is the scent of her as it grows stronger. Will she be just beyond the door? My heart tightens as I wrestle with the phantom feeling of her rushing into my arms.

I rap at the door with my fist, the doorframe shaking beneath my fury.

"Alright, alright." A muffled voice, deep with a southern drawl, comes from inside the house. It is certainly not Heather's.

The door swings open, and there's a man with green scales covering his skin, holding an ice pack to his head with webbed hands. The man squints as if hungover, blinking at the lot of us. "Howdy."

"Did the giant fish man just ... *howdy* at us?" Rosie whispers, taking a half-step behind me. I shield her; it is good enough for our mortal friends to offer their help. It is the least I can do to make sure they feel safe.

"You will get used to such things," Holly assures her in a quiet voice. Pepper flutters back to our sides. The crestfallen expression on their face tells me everything I need to know; with the way her scent has faded, I do not believe Heather is here either.

Though, this man might know something.

"Oh, Gil, it is you." Holly greets the fish man with unexpected familiarity and a small bow of her head. I do not think this man is of a noble court, but from the change in tone, I must assume he is a friend. Still, that revelation does little to calm the nerves inside me.

She was here.

"Where is my wife?" The title slips out before I realize it, but I do not take it back. We may not have gotten to our ceremony, but our love is true—rings and words are purely a gesture to the rest of the world. She is mine, and she was here.

"Come inside, y'all—I'll explain everything I know." Gil opens the door the rest of the way, allowing us entry to his home. I look to the group, who shrug in unison.

"We can trust him, brother," Holly assures me. I sigh, accepting that I must endure yet another conversation before finding my flame.

Entering Gil's home, there is a softness that takes me off guard. In a way, it reminds me of the cabin Heather and I reside in. While it has a splattering of unique decorations, it lacks the small personal details of a couple in love.

"A real firecracker, if you don't mind me saying so," Gil comments, the ice pack still resting on his head. I wonder if she's the one who gave him the blow—and what he might have done to deserve it.

"I do." I take a step closer. I cannot glean the meaning behind his tone, but I do not like it.

The rest of the group rests on a light blue sofa, but I cannot find it in me to relax, not when we were so close.

"Relax, my feathered friend." He chuckles. Gil moves through the house, getting a set of glasses, a pitcher of what appears to be lemonade, and a tin of cookies. May no one say that the Gill People are without hospitality; however, I am not looking for a host. I am looking for answers. "Your betrothed is safe, no doubt plotting a way out of her bargain…" He sets the items down on the coffee table.

"Her *what?*" Holly jumps in, rising from her place on the couch. "Gil, tell me you did *not* say the word 'bargain.'"

"Would hate to lie to you, darlin.'"

Darlin'… I bristle.

"How exactly do you two know each other?" Pepper asks the question before I have a chance.

"I shared a dance with a few of his kin some seasons ago." She shrugs but cannot hide the blush that covers her face.

"Both Finn and Goldie still speak of you." Gil smiles at her. "My siblings will be mighty jealous of this encounter, though I must admit, my affections lay elsewhere."

"Ah, yes, I remember you spent much of the ball pining for a lost love," Holly says, a smile cracking through her tough exterior. "We did manage to drag you out for a few songs."

"I didn't stand a chance against the peer pressure of you three." Gil laughs, and I relax if only slightly. Though I will not let my guard down, Holly's friendship with him seems genuine enough.

"Perhaps you've taken more after your brother than we realized," Pepper teases before raising their cup to their lips.

"Let us not get distracted!" Holly clears her throat, her face flushed. "Heather has a bargain with the vampire king—what are the terms?"

A bargain… I do not know much about them, but it does not bode well for us.

"They are bound until he finds another love or releases her," Gil says. My body tenses. How dare he bind them together in such a frivolous promise. I wish I did not doubt Heather's abilities to carry out this nonsensical matchmaking plan.

"I take it that means we cannot cause him harm?" I groan. Oh, how I crave the simplicity of the mortal realm, where claws can cut and bones can snap, without worrying about curses and bargains.

"Well, you could—but it won't break the deal unless you flat out kill 'm." He shrugs. "Wouldn't blame you."

"Is it an enchantment?" I ask. "Will it affect her safety or free will?"

"A bargain can't change a heart. Just make a mess of an already bad situation." He shakes his head, gills flaring at his sides. He points to the ice pack with webbed fingers. "I tried to reason with him, didn't go so well. We've always fought like brothers, but I've never seen him like this."

"Well, it's all very inconvenient," Holly huffs. "Why would Heather do something so foolish?"

"She didn't seem to know the words would mean anything," Gil says. Holly's brow rises as he looks at us expectedly. "Said she's new here…"

As trustworthy as he may be, an explanation is not offered.

"I am sure that, in our time together, someone must have warned her to be careful…" Holly shakes her head. "I know I have expressed the dangers of such things, haven't I?" She turns to me, and I can do nothing but shake my head.

Holly and Mother have not offered much help when it comes to navigating this world. Heather adapts too well for them to baby her, and they assume, because of my history here, I will remember customs and rules.

"I've heard you offer no more than vague threats," Pepper says under their breath, earning a glare from Holly before she softens.

"Perhaps you are right, I should have focused less on swordplay and more on … practical advice." Holly groans.

"Okay, just so I'm keeping up, you shouldn't make deals with faeries?" Rosie pipes up. The four of us nod. That much I know now.

"Have you any idea where they are?" I ask. The conversation has shifted, and I cannot allow us to lose any more time.

"Somewhere in that big spooky castle of his—but it's warded," Gil huffs. "That's Magnus for you: private, paranoid, and persistent." He looks me in the eyes. "He won't hurt her though; she's not in any danger of being more than annoyed by his prattling."

"He will still get what he deserves," I seethe, struggling to keep my composure. It sounds like this man—Gil—has done what he could to sway the vampire king. I just wish we had arrived sooner.

"Fair is fair." Gil shrugs "But remember, keeping him alive and sufferin' alone is crueler than a clean death."

"You want me to spare your friend. That is honorable." I nod. Gil seems to have sense about him, why he would be friends with the vampire king I do not know.

Still, the fate of this vampire will depend on Heather's wishes. If she wants me to cut him down I will gladly do it—either way, he will not come out of this unscathed. The thought of maiming the man who took her from me does not give me as much pleasure as the thought of her lips on mine. Getting her back is all that matters. Everything else will come second. Closing my eyes tightly, I let out a short exhale; in this moment, we are closer than we have been in days and still…

Gil takes a seat next to Rosie as if noticing her for the first time. He looks her over, his eyes widening and fins flaring as he clears his throat. "You're a human."

"And under our protection," I say, taking a spot behind her. I lay my clawed hands on her shoulder.

"Yes, yes, good but…" His face softens. "I don't presume y'all all know each other, but do you—have you ever been to Florida?"

"Just on my honeymoon," she squeaks. "Is there a reason? Or … I'm sorry, I've never met a fish person before."

"But a blonde—know any of them?"

"Um…" She looks at me and Holly as if asking for permission to give him information. We nod. I don't see how this is relevant; therefore, it cannot hurt.

"A name would be helpful." She laughs nervously running her fingers through her red hair.

"Marina." He says it like it's music, mournful and sweet, and in that moment, I know the two of us have something in common. A desperation to get back to the women we love.

Rosie shakes her head. "I'm sorry…"

"It was a long shot." He smiles, shaking his head. His gaze returns to mine. "I'll help you get back to Heather as best as I can. What do y'all need?"

"Can you get us through the wards?" I ask. If Gil is as close to the vampire king as he says, it stands to reason he would know how to reach him.

He pauses thoughtfully.

"I've been invited into his domain before. I should have access, though I can't guarantee it. Once I got this pounding to stop, I was going to take a trip to the springs and see if I can get anywhere. I suppose I can pull myself together earlier." He moves toward the door, picking up a small token that looks oddly familiar.

A gasp leaves my lips. It's a piece of that silly little Mothman keychain my flame picked up at the festival of my likeness. A smile rises on my lips. Has she truly been carrying around the token this whole time?

"This has gotta be hers, right?" Gil asks with a grin. "It's broken, but it might help us get directly to her. A personal item, recently carried, can break down wards to track someone—but I can't guarantee anything." He swings the keychain between his fingers.

And my heart leaps at the idea.

Without any further convincing, Gil dives into the water. We follow from the air, Rosie secure in my arms and holding on for dear life.

We glide past the crystal-clear water until we reach an area that is steeped in reeds and muck. He leads us to an alcove that appears to be some sort of lagoon.

It's being guarded by two gill people who wave our new friend in easily—it seems he has enough standing in this community to not be questioned. I would have thought it would be difficult to gain access to a place of magic and power.

Behind a curtain of Spanish moss, a glowing portal sits. Gil untangles something—a small key that looks like it has a thread of red hair wrapped around it. It's a gift, I assume—like giving a trusted friend a house key to water your plants when you leave town. He holds it tight, stepping into the rippling water—and *nothing.*

The surface remains as firm as glass.

"Bastard locked me out," Gil groans, knocking on the surface. It seems that, in the short time Magnus has been back in his castle, he has changed the locks.

"Let's try Heather's charm," he suggests, moving out of the way. "I'll stay back and keep an eye out—see if there's anything I can do to get through to Magnus, literally or figuratively."

"And if Heather and the vampire return here, do not let them leave," I add, regretting how sharp the command sounds when he has shown us nothing but generosity.

I am not good at this.

"I didn't intend to last time, and I won't let 'em get away again—" He offers a solemn nod, still nursing the wound on his head with ice. "If it comes to it, y'all rally the land; I'll rally the water—we don't take to getting involved with the drama of the fae folk, but… well, if I get to him first, I'll try to talk sense into him again before you beat it out of him."

"Thank you." I nod, the curt gesture a sharp contrast to his familiar way of speaking.

Holly and Gil quickly strategize: missives will be sent to the palace detailing our progress. Mother is most adept in portal travel, and while it seems old-fashioned in a world of cellphones, it will have to do.

I clutch the broken keychain in my hand, gulping as I test the waters of the portals—it gives, with the ripples and shine of magic, and hope swells in my chest.

"It appears to be working," I say, forcing myself to wait for my friends to gather at my side before jumping in alone. It is torturous, but only lasts seconds before they ready themselves and we join hands.

"She loves you something fierce," Gil says, laying a hand on my shoulder. "Magnus can't change that."

"No." I nod, sparing a glance behind me. "But it will not stop him from trying, will it?"

"I wish you luck, my friend," Gil says. "Your little firecracker will burn that whole place down if he doesn't come to his senses."

"Wouldn't that be something?" I say, thinking of the way she flickers. Watching her turn him to ash might be even more satisfying than if I were to do it myself…

Gil steps back as Rosie, Pepper, Holly and I take another step toward the portal.

"Ready?" Pepper asks.

I draw in a deep breath letting thoughts of Heather guide me. *I am coming, my flame.*

13.

Heather

"You're still here…" Magnus stands in my doorway; I can't bear to look at him from my place by the window. The shadows have shifted into countryside, with rolling mountains that span into a black fog. There's still no sunlight, and I wonder how the people in the castle get used to the way the scenery changes throughout the day. How will Moth ever find me?

Whatever the case, I don't know why Magnus would be surprised to see me here. Where else would I go? I shake my head, unwilling to look at him, not after the way he attacked Gil. It was silly to let my guard down. He's a stranger and as sad and pathetic as he seemed, maybe that's what makes him dangerous. The vampire king is fixated on me, and if he's willing to beat up his oldest friend just to keep me here, then I'm done playing this little game.

"Ah, not speaking to me now?"

Nope.

Gil's order to "make his life hell" bounces around my head. I'll need to come up with something—running won't work, neither will fighting. So, boring him with silence is my best bet. It felt different when I was only biding my time to escape. Now that I know what's going on, I can practically feel the invisible chains wrapped around me.

The thought makes a cold chill shoot through me. Moth is the only person I want my life intertwined with—but even our vows and rings would never have this kind of effect. When it comes to my cryptid fiancé, I'm his and he's mine, but Moth would never keep me against my will. Despite the rumors about the things he's done, that handsome brooding man would never, ever hurt me. He is no monster.

Which is more than I can say for Magnus.

"If I would have known you were going to run, I would not have let you out of my sight," the vampire asshole says, his voice closer now. "Despite what you may believe; I don't do this often."

I look up and watch his face change when our eyes meet. It's not longing, not even lust; there's something like a storm cloud brewing at the edge of his face, and I wish I could understand.

"I am sorry for the pain the deal caused you," he says, and it's terrible that I think he means it. I just wish he was sorry enough to let me go. He seems so far removed from the boyish image that Gil shared with me. It seems that Magnus is too far gone to reach, because I'm pretty sure blunt force trauma is more than brotherly sparring.

No, the darkness in his eyes is too deep—lost and searching before the anger returns.

"Tomorrow, when the moon rises, we will dine with my court." He nods to himself. "Considering your water-logged device is no longer operational, you will be the match I swipe right on."

I bite my tongue. If he's trying to bait me into an argument, it's not going to work. There's no way I'm going to marry him—not now, not ever.

He waits, and waits, and the room fills with his frustration. The tension between us is as thick and uncomfortable as the darkness outside the window.

"You will make an impression on the nobles here. The silent treatment ends before our meal, do you understand?" Magnus's voice is as cold as ice. It's an order; it takes every inch of my self-control not to roll my eyes.

"Do you really want to test the bounds of our deal again?" he asks, a little sharper this time. My blood goes cold. What exactly was implied in the promise I made him? So far, we've bantered and bickered, but apart from me running away, I haven't really disobeyed an order. Though, something deeper tells me this is an empty threat. The guy can't decide if he wants to be good cop or bad cop and is failing both roles.

"Goodnight to you too." He closes the door, sealing me inside; once again, I'm alone with my feelings.

I've gotten pretty good at not being on a screen before bed. Moth is an easy enough distraction, but damn, could I use an easy way to disassociate right about now. If Magnus turned out to be this fickle, what is the rest of the court going to be like? My fingers itch to scroll, to find some distraction to keep my mind off this ridiculous situation. God, I wish I had my phone...

I wish I could sneak another call to Moth—give him updates or look at his pictures. Like the one of him sipping tea in our new garden last fall, surrounded by the world's worst pumpkin patch. They refused to grow, and that's probably because Sprout napped on the garden bed every day.

But Moth—gorgeous, *gorgeous* Moth. He looks lovely in that photo, his eyes creased shut with a big fang-filled grin. Then there's the one I snapped of him in the springs of Eclipsica, shirtless and dripping with water an—*fuck*, I miss him. Without giving it a second thought, my hands begin to wander lower and lower. My fingers skillfully follow the ache that the mere memory of him stirs.

What would he say if he could see me, lying on the silk sheets in this gilded cage, burning with desire just for him? With a moan, I imagine the way his claws would feel trailing down the length of my body.

A kiss from his lips.

A bite from his fangs.

I gasp into my pillow as I find just the right spot.

My hands fist at the cold sheets, craving the warmth of his body.

That strong back.

The lines of his face.

God, I'd kiss along the strong lines of that jaw until I got to his lips. There are other things I wouldn't mind getting my lips on either.

The molten look in his ruby eyes when he's ready to pounce. I focus on the thought of him, then imagine my hands are his hands My nails sharpen.

Unable to retract the claws right away, I use my fingers to scratch my skin from hip to shoulder, gently choking myself when I reach my throat. I know he'd do it in just the right way.

I bite back a moan; the fear of being heard nearly steals the pleasure away—but I focus, imagining how Moth would talk me through it. He'd want me to feel good—to consume my thoughts and be the object of this uncontrollable desire.

I do not believe I told you to stop, he'd say. *Let them hear how much you ache for me.*

I know my body intimately enough to know just the places to touch, but while I do, I imagine it's his hand at my throat, his fingers discovering all the right ways to make me squirm.

You are so close. His lips would be on mine, stealing my breath and every last inch of restraint. I clamp my hand over my mouth and groan out his name as my limbs shake.

It was something—but I'm too needy for his touch to feel fully satisfied. I need his hands, his voice, his touch, the thought alone isn't enough to bring me to the edge. Maybe if I had a vibrator. But, even then, I'd want to feel him holding me.

I can just picture the way he'd look at me, disheveled and wanting. He'd say I was perfect, and kiss me like I'm the only one in the world. My moth, his flame. He's the only one I want, and no matter what, I'll find a way back to him. I just need to deal with my vampire problem first.

If Queen Plume's castle is like a garden, this place is a mausoleum. There is no life, no light, and no warmth. When Moth and I were first summoned to Eclipsica, this is the kind of broody, mysterious place I assumed he would have come from. But the Moth Court is filled with pastels and beautiful florals. Now, I can't picture Moth somewhere so … lifeless.

We sit at a long ornate dinner table. The tapered candles are black, of course; something I might have used back in the mortal realm as Halloween decorations.

All of the goblets are filled with red liquid—probably blood, but I'm not going to ask. The table is filled with treasures from across the realms. A serving platter spills over with pearls; gemstones are artfully displayed like candies atop a silver tray. The whole table display looks like pirate's treasure with nothing edible in sight.

Queen Plume would showcase the Moth's Court's affluence with tiny cakes and sandwiches. A noble's wealth needs to be displayed, but it's off putting to see such a literal display. I guess there's something to be said about how straightforward it is. Was it hard for them to get food delivered for me? The meals I've had here have been simple, and I wonder if that's because no one in this castle knows how to cook.

I'm served a plate of what looks like roasted vegetables and bread that I'm choosing to ignore. I can't risk having a flare up on top of being kidnapped—even though Magnus insists it's gluten-free.

We're speaking today—just barely. He's instructed me to make an impression on his court, and since I don't know the nuances of our deal, I'm doing just that.

I pick at my food even though it's the most awkward thing in the world to be the only one eating. I focus on my new mission among this court of vampires, and it's to annoy the crap out of them. It's something that I think I'm doing pretty well.

"Okay, but like… what I'm asking about with the whole blood-drinking thing is, as someone who can't ingest gluten, would I have a reaction if I drank blood from someone who just ate like a whole loaf of bread?" I ask for the third time, because the vampire king may have told me to make an impression on the court, but he didn't specify what kind.

Still, I watch Magnus hold back laughter. Rude. He's supposed to be just as annoyed as the rest of them, not entertained. Though I will say it's *interesting* to see the vampire king in public, surrounded by his court. I hadn't looked at him with anything other than contempt or curiosity over the past few days, and now that I can see him without the mask of trying to impress me, I realize how … sunken he is. His shoulders bend beneath the burden of a kingdom that has relied on him for a century. His usually hungry eyes seem blank—until, that is, I start to speak.

"When you are turned, we will source only the finest blood for you, my darling," Magnus assures me, and I cringe. This man loves to put on a show, and right now, I'm still a co-star.

"Are you familiar with the wedding customs in our domain, Heather?" a noblewoman asks. She has pale skin and dark hair with the bangs cut into a sharp V-shape across her forehead. Like everyone in this room, she's stunning and avoids looking me directly in the eye. I think I heard someone call her Cassandra.

"Oh em gee, no, I just thought I'd wing it," I say in my best valley girl voice, spreading my wings for emphasis and—*wow, they can't stand me*—heck *I can't stand me right now either.* Magnus chuckles despite himself, and I would be glad one of us is having a good time if I didn't hate his guts. Still, that connection between us buzzes; setting him up with a wife is the task on my to-do list that irks me at all hours of the day. If only he would take it seriously.

"My darling bride and I still have not gone over the details of the ceremony," Magnus says, nonchalantly leaning back in his dining chair. "As you know, many of the preparations have been made while she was away."

"Ah yes, you certainly have been kept under lock and key this past year, have you not?" Cassandra says, her dark lips pressing into a pout. "How lovely of our king to pull you into the darkness with us."

"Yeah, so lovely," someone from the end of the table pipes up, clearly not amused by the way I've been dominating the conversation. I'm glad my plan is working on someone. "Whatever the case, we must thank you, Lady Heather, for bringing our king out of hiding. It is rare to be this close to such untouchable beauty."

I cast a glance toward Magnus; I thought he'd be the type to need regular doses of flattery daily like a medication, but the smile on his lips is uncomfortable. These are not his friends—they're his subjects. With how casual the inner circle of the Moth Court is with each other, maybe I've forgotten that there's a difference.

"It will be a night to remember," Magnus agrees, and my stomach drops. He still wants to do this. What is it going to take for him to swipe left on me? I've barely glanced at him all day and still, he looks at me like I'm sunlight. Delighted, enamored, and maybe a little afraid. If only I could figure out a way to make that fear grow.

The conversation shifts, and God, I can't keep up. Have you ever started an episode of *The Bachelor* in the middle of a season? Yeah, that's what this conversation has been like. I don't bother to smile and nod along like I did when trying to mingle with the Moth Court. Instead, I allow myself to look utterly bored. Finally, I stand from the table, the chair scraping behind me.

"I'm just—"

They stare, waiting for whatever words will justify my behavior. It's probably not good form to leave a royal dinner party without asking to be excused or bowing to the king, but considering I'm trying to make them hate me, I don't bother with either.

I finally land on, "Going to get some air."

"I'll accompany you," Magnus says, rising from the head of the table.

"Or you could not." It comes out sharper than the sarcasm I was aiming for. I shoot Magnus a look; perhaps a little sass in front of his court might get him to call off this whole thing.

"Come, my king, surely you can allow your princess a moment to herself before your lifetime together," another one of the ladies—Sabella—says. Her hair flows down her back in soft waves and is the color of violets. She's been pleasant, laughs at Magnus's jokes, and is clearly into him. He's a catch around here—*why keep me?*

She places her hand on top of Magnus's, and her painted red lips lift in a smile he doesn't return. Magnus doesn't flinch, but after a long moment, he finally nods.

"Of course. Enjoy your walk, my love." The fang-filled smile does not reach his eyes.

I don't understand why he hesitates; it should be easy to let me go when he knows I have no way to escape or contact the outside world. My phone is still totally dead, though I'm not giving up hope yet. I trudge out of the dining room, relaxing only when the feeling of being watched fades. I fiddle with the Mothman keychain—well part of it. I have to guess sometime in the misadventures of The Dragonfly Court and the swamp it snapped in half. Still, a piece of the charm is still here. I've been hiding it in my pockets; thankful it stayed put amongst all the splashing yesterday.

To say the castle is large is an understatement. Though no matter where I go, I'm still close enough to Magnus for the terms of the bargain to be met. It's all dark stone and burgundy carpet, and I wonder if Magnus has my closet filled with things in cream and blush just to stand out against the dour backdrop.

A light shining in the darkness.

I cringe. The whole thing makes me feel like some kind of doll wandering around a gothic dream house. It's fairly devoid of people, though occasionally, I'll hear the clipping of heels against stone and turn to see a maid hurrying from task to task.

They look upon me with interest, and I can't blame them for being curious. It seems most of their tasks revolve around the great vampire king's wedding—and I am his bride, whether I like it or not. There's no way I'll say "I do," but the seriousness of this whole situation makes my chest heave.

We're tied together in some sick way because—*what*? I wanted to be clever? To help him? Let's face it, Magnus was never serious about online dating. He's humored me to bide his time until the wedding.

I'm a fool.

My head is spinning, fixating on all the things I've done wrong. I blink, and the edges of the room begin to blur until everything is the color of blood. I close my eyes tight, steadying myself on the edge of the staircase. Feathers poke out of the skin on my arms and—*what the hell?*

I throw myself through the first door I find.

A bedroom.

The mirrors are cracked and covered by sheets. It reminds me, in a way, of Queen Plume's collection of broken clocks, and doesn't seem grand enough for a king to rest his head. The portal that's glowing in the corner, however, suggests this room belongs to Magnus. I would have expected it to be under lock and key. Maybe it's warded just like everything else in this damn castle—enchanted to let me through in hopes I'd end up in his bed one day—as if. The anger and tension swell at the base of my shoulders. I throw myself toward the rippling surface, only to be met with the hard press of glass against my shifting skin. *I'm never going to find a way out.* I think, and the quiet darkness fills with sound of my cracking bones. My figure grows as my body morphs painful and strange until painted in shadow is a silhouette I don't recognize.

Oh my God…

Straightening my back, I gaze into one of the cracked, gilded mirrors—my reflection stretched and shattered in the broken glass.

My face is still mine, but everything else—well I'm not exactly sure what I'm seeing. Combing my fingers through my hair, the texture is more akin to feathers. It's soft like the way Moth feels when he's transformed. The long strands hang down my back, aside from unruly bangs shooting out around my antenna.

When I move, my feet—my talons—scrape the stone floor emitting a sound that makes my teeth hurt. I move closer to my reflection, taking in the details. My eyes have taken on a strange milky green hue, the same shade as my wings. Other than that, I'm unrecognizable, half-shifted into a monster. Feathers poke from my skin, and my cream-colored dress is tattered, half of the garment in a pile on the floor. A hard exoskeleton covers my body from legs to chest.

The door creaks open. I see the shadow before anything else—a dark, looming figure creeping up behind me. Whirling around, it's the blade that catches my attention first, short with gems encrusted from the handle to the tip. It's gripped in Magnus's shaking hands. His unblinking eyes stare at me with no recognition. It's as if he's afraid…

"Don't step any closer!" His usually smooth voice is just as cracked as the mirrors in this room. Motionless, we stare at one another, his gaze rising from my claws to my face.

"Heather?" He blinks, searching every inch of me. With a clank, the blade falls to the ground and he stumbles back. "You're, you're—"

Red swims at the corner of my eyes, and when I open my mouth to speak, a growl replaces anything of substance.

"Heather. *Darling*—"

I want to hurt him.

And I think I just might.

Moth

THE CABIN.

We are back at the cabin.

I imagine her lounging on our loveseat, a book in her hand. She kisses my lips and tells me her scheme worked. She has been waiting for me to return. But we search, and search, bickering and talking over each other— she's not here.

Surrounded by her scent and wedding decorations, my compatriots and I lay together on the floor, displaced and discontented. The open portal glows by the bookcase, lighting our way back to Eclipsica. I am thankful my mother-in-law appears to have stepped out. Her minivan is not in the drive, and for now, the space is ours to wallow in.

If any of us dares to speak to Pepper, they just groan. Heather calls this *'rotting'*—when your body simply will not allow you to do anything else. Perhaps it has been too much failure for us to bear.

"Friends, we *must* strategize," Holly says, though she sounds exhausted. "She was under my watch. I am fighting the urge to run off on my own to fix things."

"We were all right there," Rosie reminds her. "I know I don't have powers or anything like that, but we were all right there—and, *and*… what if we can't find her? I mean, those portals, do you even understand how they work? It should have led us to her, right?"

It is correct for her to be upset. She is giving voice to every horrible thought I have had since the portal lead us back here.

"Enough," I groan, but my racing thoughts do not settle down even in silence. I need her back with me. "Our focus should be on finding a way to break the bond. Is it possible without the vampire king's cooperation?"

Holly shakes her head. "The magic that seals things like that is binding to your very soul—"

"Damn, it's bad enough that Heather is missing. Magic binding her soul sounds … concerning." Rosie groans. "What are we going to do?"

A cool draft blows into the room, followed by the scent of coffee. Picking up my head from when it has fallen onto the cushions, I glance up to see our front door is open and my future mother-in-law is standing in the doorway, holding a large coffee in her hands. By the way her mouth is hanging open, I wonder just how long she's been standing there—

"Oh my God." Her voice is understandably shrill. "Oh my God, oh my God, oh my God!"

We have not bothered to hide or shift into human forms—and we all seem to be frozen in place by her unexpected appearance. She is lucky. Normally, when Holly is startled, she reaches for her sword, but instead, she clambers for her glamour. It is too little too late. There's no use hiding it.

The wings, however, seem to be the least of Marsha's worries as she closes in on me. Heather has always said she and her mother look very little alike, but I see a striking resemblance in the fire of their eyes.

Swallowing hard, I kick myself for not letting her in on this sooner. If there is anyone who would burn the world to get someone back, it's a mother looking for their child.

"Where would you like me to begin?" I ask, glancing around the room. "I fear we do not have time for all the details but—"

"Uh, you could start by explaining why it looks like I just walked into a room filled with extras from a low-budget fantasy movie!" Her eyes dart around the room, and I do not know whether she is going to begin shouting or simply faint with the way her face is turning red. "Or maybe focus on the fact that *no one told me* my little girl is missing!"

"What is a fantasy movie?" Pepper whispers to Holly, whose face has gone pale.

"A pornography, I presume," she whispers back, a little more than offended. Meanwhile, Rosie bites back a laugh.

I narrow my eyes in their direction. Now is not the time. Not when this small woman looks like she is going to explode.

"What are you hiding, hm?!" She jabs me in the chest.

So, I tell her.

Everything. Everything that Heather had been waiting for the right time to let her in on, guilt seeping into me with every word. But if not now, then when? We have been running in circles and are no closer to the end.

She should know what the situation is—and how dire I fear it is becoming.

We sit together, not bothering with the formality of gathering at the table or brewing a pot of tea. The coffee she brought home goes untouched as I honestly tell her everything I can. The way I fell onto her daughter's roof, the way Heather aided me, the truth of my origins and my history on this mortal plane and outside of it. She just listens, except for an occasional 'hmm', her brow furrowed. That is, until I explain our failed attempt to find Heather through the portal that sent us here.

"Buffering" is what Heather would call it. The room is silent until Marsha finally nods, grabbing for her coffee that has gone cold and taking several gulps.

"So, let me get this straight, you're royalty from another world?" Her eyebrows pinch together, and mouth in a straight unamused line.

"Yes."

"And… and some fancy rich vampire just stole my daughter? Days before her wedding?"

"Also correct," I reply, trying and failing to keep the defeat from both my tone and my shoulders.

"And my daughter's response to this ridiculous situation is to set up her kidnapper with a dating profile?" Marsha is shouting now. It is not an unreasonable reaction. "*And* you're telling me her soul is bound to him with some kind of … spell?"

"That is the gist of it." Holly groans from her spot behind me. "But as far as a rich vampire, King Magnus is not as well-to-do as some would think. When he accepted the invitation to last year's ball, he showed up in clothes from three seasons ago with hunger in his eyes. His kingdom is in all but ruin, and he wants a rich faerie royal to ease his troubles."

"You think he kidnapped her for money?" Rosie asks. "There must be something more to the story here. Moth is the one who's a prince."

"Please." Marsha snorts. "Heather was the internet's princess for years. I made some mistakes oversharing her personal life, but every cent she made was put into savings. She did well enough to buy this place." She leans against the doorway, and a piece of trim splinters, leaving her stumbling.

"Indeed." Pepper's brow pinches. "And as lovely as it may be, the vampire king's actions will have consequences."

"To say the least," I reply with honesty, flexing my claws reflexively. I am glad when Marsha does not seem afraid. "We just need to find her first."

"But she's safe, right?" Marsha asks, her voice rising into something more frantic. "Please tell me she's safe."

"Yes, we have no reason to believe the vampire king would hurt her," Holly replies, her eyes cast to the floor for a moment. "During the brief conversation she had with Moth, she assured us as much."

Marsha lets out a long sigh, easing herself into one of the armchairs.

"Trying to help this guy, it's very on-brand for Heather," Marsha says. "She's always been too worried about hurting people's feelings, even when she'd get attacked by trolls, she'd always say they must be having a worse day than she was."

"Must we add *trolls* to the list of foes to contend with?" Holly sighs, shaking her head. "My sister-in-law has seen many battles."

I open my mouth, debating on whether or not to explain what a troll is in terms of the internet, but Rosie looks my way and shakes her head. We simply do not have the time.

"So, you're all on this noble quest, hopping through portals, doing God-knows-what." Marsha exhales. She shakes her head, pulling a bright pink cellphone from her pocket. "And you don't know where she's being held at all?"

"For all we know, she isn't even in the faerie realms at all," I admit. "The fact she was able to call suggests that if she isn't in the mortal realm, the veil is thin where she is."

"Then I'll handle this." Marsha holds her phone as if it is a weapon. Her thumbs skillfully fly across her keyboard, typing and typing until—"There!"

She hands me the phone, revealing a post on Heather's social media account.

<*@HoneyBeaLatte: Hey Everyone! In the past few years, I've been talking a lot about my life online, but I've been noticing this trend of people filming and photographing strangers and posting them without permission. That's why I want to do an experiment. If you see me out in public this week, snap a candid and hashtag #TheresHoneyLatte to raise awareness on this social phenomenon. Since going off the grid, I obviously haven't shared my home, and I have been traveling so I could be anywhere—but if I know anything about you Honey Bees, you will be too! So, good luck and I am both terrified and excited to see what I'm tagged in next week."* >

I grimace. Heather would hate this, but it may work. She's been tagged in countless unflattering photos over the years, and the lack of privacy is something she has spoken about before, so it's not exactly left field. Still, I believe her followers will find it … odd.

"Wait, wait, wait," Rosie says, lunging for the phone. "You have your daughter's passwords? That's not okay!"

"Do you think that's the biggest problem we have to focus on right now?" Marsha says, crossing her arms, keeping the device tightly in her hand. "Yes? Okay! And no, I do not log in to spy on her. She's had some of these accounts since she was a teenager, and I'm still one of the recovery emails—and would you stop looking at me like that?"

"This will bode results?" I ask, noting that while this may not be the "biggest problem," it will be addressed as soon as this crisis is handled. However, we cannot just keep sitting and waiting.

"It will get people talking and looking, which is what we need." She sighs. "If we're lucky, some news outlets will pick it up—I *just* reposted from my account which will help."

"And then you will log out—change the passcodes and be done with this," I say firmly and, begrudgingly, Marsha agrees. In the meantime, we gather around the small screen watching the post climb in popularity in a matter of minutes.

"Your world and ours seem to have one thing in common," Holly says, her pupils dilated as she stares transfixed by the tiny screen.

"And what is that?" Marsha asks as her fingers slide across the keys.

"The love of drama."

"If it's one thing I know it's this," Marsha says, addressing the whole room now, "she'll be home in no time."

15.

Heather

I WANT TO LASH OUT WITH MY CLAWS AND cut through the ghostly pale flesh of his neck. With a deep breath, I steady myself with a deep breath; every inch of me starts to shake as I fight against my instincts. I don't know how our deal works.

If I hurt *him*—what will happen to *me*?

Another growl erupts from my lips as I fight against the urge to slice through him. Exhaustion builds as the room goes from red to black to red to black.

The way my bones push and pull inside my body makes me curl in on myself, and I collapse onto the floor. Still shifted, I shake, balling my talon-tipped hands into fists.

I could tear every inch of this castle down, and it still wouldn't be enough.

"Deep breath—in and out," Magnus urges. "The anger isn't you, sweet Heather. Listen to my voice."

I stare up at him, trying to blink the red from my eyes. As much as I want to give into my frustration, I can't let myself do anything I'm going to regret, and with the way I'm already shaking with exhaustion…

"Now, think of a place—something to ground you— where you can let your armor fall and just be yourself." Images flicker through my mind: Moth and I lying in bed or relaxing on the couch. But, even after two years, the vision of Chris with rope in his hands creeps back into my head. Scales and feathers poke out of my skin, and my jaw becomes so tight I worry it'll stretch into a beak.

It fucking hurts. Worse than the tension I feel when my wings are hidden beneath my skin. Under the calm surface, is this what shifting feels like for Moth too? He always makes it so easy and—ah! The feeling of bones expanding makes me double over. I pat my dress, searching for my fragmented Mothman keychain as something to comfort me and find nothing. My head continues to spin with memories I can't forget. The smell of sawdust suddenly overwhelms everything else.

"Please—focus, darling." Magnus's voice snaps me back to the reality. The two of us alone in his bedroom. Another captor who thinks they know what's best for me.

This is me, and it's not, and I don't know what to do. Panic grips my lungs as my face begins to contort, then settle, and shift again.

"*Not there*," he says. It would sound like an order if it wasn't so panicked. I shake my head, the fear and anger building over and over again. Where would I go, if I could be anywhere right now? "You need to picture a place where you can let your armor fall and just be yourself."

The field of flowers.

The first place that felt like a date.

I breathe in the scent, remembering the way his body looked sprawled out among the blooms. The sharp contrast of Moth's claws as he stroked the petals made it all that much more appealing.

The scent of garden mums and canna lilies tickle my nose as soft blades of grass graze the backs of my thighs. I think and focus and dream of that small slice of heaven that feels so much like home.

The place where I knew for sure I loved Moth and I hoped he would love me back.

Our lips touched, soft and sweet, with a need to be filled for the rest of our lives. His body and mine among the flowers, hands and mouths entertained for as long as faeries live.

I'll never tire of him.

As I breathe sharply, I am dimly aware of the sensation of shrugging off the weight of an oversized sweater—I am lighter but so very cold. Magnus grips my hand and I pretend with everything in me that it's Moth.

"That's it." Magnus's voice is a cruel reminder that I'm a world away from my future husband.

I let go of his hand in an instant, and my body begins to collapse into itself. The warmth of Magnus's heavy black cloak falls over my shoulders before skin replaces my feathers, and I'm thankful for the sliver of modesty. As my legs shake, I wrap the garment around myself. But I'm still raging—my arms covered in feathers, and my eyes bursting with fireworks.

"There… your beauty restored."

"You're such a—" I whisper, unable to finish the sentence before sleep takes me. *Asshole.*

When I wake up, I'm in the same room. Fresh clothing and a tray of food sits at the bedside, and, to my relief, I'm alone. The cloak is still wrapped around me, which suggests Magnus carefully moved me to the bed without being a creep. Still, I slip into the yellow chemise that's been laid out on a chair.

Everything hurts.

Is it like this when Moth shifts? He always changes shape effortlessly, but I feel like I just pounded three margaritas and then tried to do CrossFit.

I reach for the tray of food, confident by this point that the food isn't poisoned. Sitting cross-legged in bed, I eat.

I don't think I liked, well… *any of that*. The new shape of my body—though powerful and comfortable—was overshadowed by the sharp rage that threatened to eat through me with every passing second. If Magnus hadn't talked me down, I might have actually hurt him. God, I wanted to—and kinda wish I had.

But when the insufferable vampire king arrives to check on me, he's holding a cup of that pink-tinted almond tea. I debate for a moment on whether to tell him to go away. I'm not above kicking him out of his own bedroom if I have to…

"How did you learn to do that?" I ask, unable to help myself. "To change back, I mean…"

"I cannot take credit for the tea, one of the maids brewed it at my request and—" He rambles, setting the tea cup on the end table.

"I'm talking about shifting back…" I clarify because he wouldn't have been able to talk me through that frazzled guided meditation without at least some experience. I look at the area his wings should be. "Was it before you started wearing a glamour?"

He steps backward. I can't help but notice that he's keeping his distance, and the extra breathing room is a nice change of pace.

"The sight of … abnormalities among my kind is not exactly celebrated," he said, fiddling with his necklace; it must be his glamour. "Neither court enjoyed looking upon them. Their sneers of distain were enough motivation to learn. Was this your first time?"

"I've done minor things before, but nothing like that," I answer honestly. There's no use trying to hide it. I've seen his wings and know he's either hiding them or using a glamour. It seems unfair that it's something his court won't accept. As pissed as I am, I'll admit they're pretty—and the color matched his violet eyes perfectly.

He's essentially photoshopping himself because of comments he's received his whole life—and damn, if that's not something I can sympathize with.

"You probably have more experience," I say, eyeing him. Is there a version of him he loathes even more than this? Something that might actually be worth breaking mirrors over?

"Even still, I have never…" He swallows hard. "If I have a form like yours—I would not want to know it."

"Seriously?" I snap. "No offense, but you seem like the type who would want more power, not less."

"I do not want to offend."

"As if anything you could say would make me hate you more." I cross my arms as an uncomfortable feeling washes over me. I realize it's *his* bed I've taken over.

"Beauty is power," he says with a small shrug, as if it's not something to be debated. "I have never found the forms the Moths and Bumbles take … appealing. I've made it clear your aesthetics, shall we say, are one of the reasons I've been drawn to you."

"Is that why when I turned back you said my beauty had been restored?" I ask, and he simply nods.

"Don't you think that's shallow? Like, think about it. If we do find some mortal to set you up with, she'll grow old. Marriage is in sickness and health——"

"Mortal vows are meaningless in the world of faeries and monsters. The woman in question would become a vampire." He sighs. "I'm sure your fiancé would agree with the sentiment."

"Considering we were about to have a mortal wedding——no, I don't think he would," I huff. Moth would accept me no matter what. I *know* that.

"He turned you, didn't he?" Magnus says, and though he's still keeping his distance, his gaze is dagger sharp.

"He didn't have a choice," I bristle. "I told you; this isn't my first time being kidnapped."

"What happened the first time, Heather?" he asks, closer now.

"None of your business!" I cut him off, my claws sharpening into points. He reaches out, but falls short of actually touching me. Still, there's a seriousness about him I'm not used to. *Protective.*

"But if there was another suitor——someone who you still pine for——someone your fiancé hurt." Magnus's sentences are choppy as he tries to work out the details of my past. Unfortunately the clueless vampire king is once again using a set of pieces that don't belong to the right game. He's right that someone stole me away from Moth——but it wasn't something I wanted, and neither is this.

Rage boils in my chest.

"Look, I understand being kidnapped by a faerie is some kind of problematic Old World form of flattery here, but he was a human. It was not romantic—it was terrible, and invasive, and he broke into my house, okay?!" The rant bursts from my lips, and I close my arms protectively around my chest. "Normally, being stolen away in the night is a fucking bad thing, okay?"

"Yes, but you are unhappy, aren't you?" He blinks—and he really is stuck on that, isn't he? "I saw the far away stare you wore when you stood next to your betrothed. One my presence replaced with a smile. This rescue was for your well-being."

"My first kidnapper thought it was for my own good too. He thought Moth had some kind of mind control over me," I say, touching the places on my wrist where I still remember being bound with rope. "He used me for bait to try to catch Moth, okay? I was tied up in a damn barn like a piece of meat and—and—" Tears burn my eyes too fast for me to blink them away.

"Is that why you thought I had captured you? To get to him?" he asks.

"Yeah."

"And now you're here."

"Now I'm here," I echo, wishing I could just become numb to this whole thing.

"I do not want you to feel that pain again—" Magnus says in a low voice I suppose he intends to be reassuring. "You cannot be taken again while cloaked in the shadows or at my side. I promise I will keep you safe from every threat."

"You *are* the threat."

He draws back as if wounded, shaking his head.

"I know you said the tower was your refuge—but mine is a cabin in the woods surrounded by trees—with the man

I love," I admit. God, am I just too exhausted to have a filter? I shouldn't be telling him any of this. Maybe it's the bargain chipping away at my resolve but I can't stop myself. "I need to get back to Moth and tell him about all this shifting stuff. He'll know what to do."

"In time, you'll be able to suppress that form."

"The rage? Sure, hopefully." I shrug. "Everything else, I think might just be a part of adjusting to all of this. Most of the Moth region can transform on command so I guess, one day, I'll probably be able to…"

"But why would you want to?" Magnus makes a face, I know he's all about aesthetics or whatever, but could he take a break from being shallow until the end of this conversation?

"That's really close-minded of you." I run my fingers through the soft waves of my hair, remembering how they felt as downy feathers.

"It would be a disservice to deprive you of my honesty." He shrugs.

"But you can deprive me of my freedom?" I shoot back, glaring. If we have one more circular conversation, I'm going to scream.

"Touché." His reply is paired with a wince, and I wonder if I'm actually getting somewhere. Though, knowing Magnus, it's doubtful.

"What about Gil?" I ask, still stuck on this obsession with beauty.

Magnus tenses, the way you would if I had spoken poorly about a family member.

"Heather, now is hardly the time. I will send for your clothing, some water, and we will get you into—"

"Gil. Is he beautiful?" I press.

"For all intents and purposes, he is a giant fish person." He laughs, and his fingers brush the hair away from his face in a movement that looks *nervous.* "You should see his glamour; in skin, he is the strangest of things."

What a rude thing to say about a friend, and worst of all, I can tell he thinks it's true. I fight with myself, unsure of what is a thought and what's said out loud. I want to tell Magnus not everything has to be beautiful to have value—and I get how rich that is coming from someone who buys impractical kitchen appliances just because they're pretty. But doesn't he know that there's beauty in everything?

"Now that we are speaking…" Magnus says, his expression turning sheepish. "I have something else to ask you."

"Great," I groan.

"Tell me what was wrong with the date. Tell me how to fix it." He sits next to me like we're teenagers gossiping instead of… *whatever the hell is going on here.*

I frown. How can I be strategic with whatever conversation is about to happen? Despite cracking through Magnus's surface, he still has no intention of letting me go. Even if I can't escape—I can *maybe* change the playing field.

"I mean, that was lovely, but you'll probably have to start smaller if you're dating a mortal."

"Smaller?" Magnus's eyes dance with curiosity. "Where would you suggest?"

"Can we go anywhere?"

"As long as it is with me, of course."

"Then take me to a portal. If you're going to date a human, we should practice in my realm," I conclude.

"You are persistent but exhausted. Rest, then I will take you wherever you desire," he says, and my heart leaps.

"I think you're wrong about Gil, by the way. He was charming." I hate to admit it, but Magnus is right. Even though I just woke up, I feel like I could sleep for a week. "I hope things work out with him and Marina."

"Love between a creature and a human—do you really think it would work?" His voice is far away now.

"Of course I do." I smile as I twist the engagement ring on my finger. "I'm in love with Mothman."

Moth

I PACE AND PACE AND PACE UNTIL I FEAR A hole will bore into the floor. My mother-in-law gazes at me with an expression that hinges on anger and sympathy.

It is just the two of us now—three counting my trusted hound who appears to have taken the shape of a throw pillow, fitting as this is a moment for rest.

Our party has regrouped, traded information, and now for the moment rest our heads in the worlds we have chosen. Rosie and Clara have gone home for the night—it is up to them whether they want to join us for this madness in the morning. It is no secret the exhaustion of our failing quest is taking a toll, and I am glad to have a moment free from the memories the castle holds.

Holly has returned to relieve Pepper of their position and give them much needed time with their family. An ordeal like this does make a person—or faerie—want to hold their loved ones close, and Ruby and Pepper have so many to tuck into bed and tell bedtime stories to. Mother and Holly will have things handled in the castle in the meantime. For now, a portal remains open in the living room, and I wish Heather would be the next to step through it.

For now, our task is to rest before morning, and I am glad my friends can return to their quiet lives. But it seems like the way Marsha's eyes are fixed on mine, I still have some chaos I must contend with.

"Why didn't she tell me?" she finally asks, falling onto the old loveseat next to Sprout, who wastes no time snuggling his head onto her lap.

"She wanted to," I admit. "It has not been an easy task to figure out the timing."

"Did she think I wouldn't accept her? I bought her a rainbow flag when she was twelve for God's sake..."

"And shared it online for everyone to see." I can understand my flame's hesitation to share any personal details of her life and identity with her mother. The things we have experienced are fantastical in the mortal realm, and their relationship, though healing, still has moments of strain. Marsha has done well to accept the changes Heather has made since coming to these woods, but it has not come without effort.

It is hard to share secrets when you are still closing wounds from the past.

"That's—okay, yes. That was pretty bad—*really* bad." She frowns, sinking into herself. "There are so many things I wish I could do over."

"What I'm trying to say is... all of this, I accept it," Marsha says with not a flicker of doubt in her eyes. "Just tell me what your crest and colors are, and I'll be the first to cross-stitch them onto a set of linens for your eyes only. I just want her back."

"As do I." I nod. "I can answer any of your basic questions but, as you may have gathered, I do not recall much of my life before coming to the mortal realm."

"Really?" she says, leaning back as the pieces click into place. "I figured you dodging all my questions meant you were in the witness protection program or just didn't like me…"

"The truth is unfortunately more complicated."

"Mothman, huh?" Marsha appraises me.

"Your daughter gave me my name—*Moth*—unrelated to that title."

"I just thought it was short for something…"

"What could it possibly be short for?" I ask, momentarily ceasing my pacing to pivot toward her.

"Timothy?"

"Ti-moth-y?" Unexpected laughter quakes from my chest. Sleep will not come easily tonight, but it is needed. Especially if I am to continue to converse with my mother-in-law—as entertaining as this exchange might be.

"Okay, okay." She extends her hands. "Don't be mad, but I may have asked my followers what a full name for Moth might be—just a quick insta story, and I deleted it once I got enough replies. Nameberry barely gave me any results and Heather said it wasn't a nickname. I don't know, I just know so little about you…"

"And your followers suggested … Ti-moth-y?" I shake my head but can't help but laugh at the strangeness of, well, this whole thing. I suppose there is something natural about having a curiosity for someone your daughter is about to marry.

She shakes her head. "Well, whatever the case, I may have not known what my daughter was marrying into, but I like your mom. Plume is nice—wait, should I address her more formally?"

"I think first names will suffice—we will all be family soon."

If we can get Heather back.

"Well mother-in-laws don't always get along, historically-speaking," she begins. I raise an eyebrow; I was unaware of that. "And I think we are going to make an excellent team."

Why does that idea cause terror to swell in my veins?

"And she's single, right? You know, I have a brother. Very quirky, tall, he's coming to the wedding and I'm sure—"

"I have met Heather's uncle, yes," I cut her off before she can continue. When we met at the festival of my likeness last year, he seemed upstanding, and well-adored by Heather...

"You were in the other realm when he arrived for the wedding. Clara set him up with a bunch of projects around their farm to keep him busy. He's a good guy, a little quiet." She fidgets with her phone. "I've always wanted him to find someone kind he can depend on—"

"If it is all the same to you, I do not have the energy to play matchmaker for my mother this evening." The mention of matchmaking sets my flesh on edge remembering the fool's errand my flame has taken upon herself.

"Right, I'll take care of everything." Marsha raises her cellphone with such speed it is dizzying.

"Marsha, *please*." I pinch my brow, not wishing to engage in this conversation anymore.

"What? I need a distraction! It's not every day your daughter is taken by a... did you all say he's a *vampire?*"

"He is." I nod. "Holly has advised that we regroup—relax even. That seems unfathomable."

"You're telling me. You don't even get Bravo out here and, no offense, the Wi-Fi is horrendous." She sighs, looking at our ancient television set. "I've seen old TVs like this before. Honey always said she wanted one, but I figured she'd gut it and put something with an Apple TV inside."

"No offense taken."

I think Heather purposely downgraded with the knowledge that her mother would soon be coming to town.

"And, I have heard of the cocktail but do not understand what relevance or function it would have in this context."

"Huh?" She blinks.

"An apple—tini…" I repeat. "Is that not what you said?"

To my surprise, Marsha doubles over laughing. What is humorous about "gutting" a television to put an alcoholic beverage inside?

"I don't think a breakdown of streaming services is going to help us this evening, especially when there's none here to use as examples." She shakes her head. "But God, you're just the cutest thing, aren't you? And we're lucky: even with this Wi-Fi situation, I was able to make that post." She sighs. "Took forever to go through, but it's already getting a little bit of traction."

"And you truly think it will work?" I ask, ignoring the strange feeling that I have been complimented and insulted all at the same time.

She says nothing, dropping the bravado she had when she announced her plan to the group.

"I don't know, Moth. But I can't just sit around and do nothing." It is not the certainty I had hoped for. "You have your world, and this is mine. All I can do is what I know and hope Heather doesn't hate me for it."

"She will not." I nod. "If anything, she may commend the craftiness of your plan. I do. Though, the fact you gained access to her accounts is…"

"Not great—I know, I know!" She shows me her device, pulling up screens I cannot decipher the meaning of. "As soon as this is done, I'll scrub this thing clean, but on the off chance someone sends a DM with information that could help… I promise I haven't been poking around here randomly."

"I will trust you on that." I nod. "It is good to have so many people who care for Heather and are willing to offer their help." *While I sit and do nothing.*

"You realize all these people love you too, don't you?" The words strike me like a sword to the chest. "They're not just doing this to help Heather—they're here for you too."

I pause.

Love. Of course. It's something they have all expressed—though, sometimes, with teasing—but I had not stopped to realize that my friends are not worried about what my claws will do; they care for my well-being.

"It is a strange thing," I manage to say, realizing Marsha is staring intently as if waiting for a response. "Over the last few days, I have had to contend with the idea of leaning on Heather or these new friends. There is a feeling of weakness in it, a feeling that because I cannot do it all myself, I am not enough."

"You've been alone for a long time." She nods. "We're both relearning how to connect, huh? As you pointed out earlier, I haven't always been the best mom to her." She brings the conversation back to her, something that would surely annoy Heather, but I am thankful for. "I've been selfish. I'm sure you've heard all about the ways I told Heather's stories—every little embarrassing detail of her childhood is on my blog. I was so clouded by building my brand, my community, that I didn't realize the impact it would have on her as an adult. I always wanted her to follow in my footsteps, but I'm glad to see what she's built out here with you. Her new art pieces have been stunning. I don't think she would have gotten there without logging off the way she did."

"She is a talent." I should like to get some of the images she's made framed rather than be forced to enjoy them on such a small digital screen.

"She sure is." Marsha smiles wistfully. "It was always just us in our little bubble—until she got old enough to start reading the comments. I suppose 'don't feed the trolls' probably has another meaning in your realm, huh?"

"I suppose it must." I sink into one of the kitchen chairs, realizing I cannot adequately have this conversation while pacing.

"It must be hard not to remember everything," she says, a sadness on her face. "So many gaps to try to fill in…"

"It feels as if I am supposed to recover them to move on." I shake my head. "But, memories I can make more of—as long as they have my flame in them, I will be content."

"*Your flame.*" She giggles. "Look, you're going through a rebrand. We've all been there. You don't need to remember who you were to become the person you want to be."

Weight eases from my chest. I now understand why Heather calls this woman a few times a week to chat despite their complicated relationship. Unwillingly, I am finding it easy to be candid with her.

"I'm glad you two found each other. Even if it feels like she's farther away than ever…"

"The faerie realm is—"

"No, before this." She sighs. "I know it's my fault for breaking her trust. Some days it just feels like it's going to take my whole life to earn it back."

"But still, you are here." I nod, unsure of what else to say to her in this moment. Heather has spoken at length about what damage growing up in the spotlight has done. It is not as if it was something she was born into—everything her mother shared online was a choice. Marsha has changed a lot in a very short time. But seeing how quickly she was able to hack into her daughter's accounts to post this "test" was eerie.

"You mentioned the post has gotten … more traction?" I ask, not meaning to change the subject. She hesitates but passes me the phone. A feed of blurry photos tagged with Heather's alias is laid out before me. I cringe. Heather is right to be paranoid; there are photos of us in the mix. Subconsciously, I feel myself shrinking at the sight of the two us of at the festival of my likeness in Point Pleasant. I'm fully transformed and Heather, like always, is stunning.

"Those wings are actually hers, huh?" Marsha asks, blinking rapidly.

"Beautiful, are they not?"

She swallows hard. "And that's—"

"Me. Yes." I frown as her jaw drops.

She finally lands on, "I didn't think you could get taller…" before choking out a strange laugh. "The rest of the results are nothing worth mentioning. A few more interesting photos of the pair of you spotted in public, but that's not exactly going to help us, is it?"

Except as a reminder to not get lost in myself again. The last thing we need is another monster hunter showing up at our door. I stand, unable to sit still for a moment longer. I itch to spread my wings and claws but cannot risk being seen.

The vampire is enough to contend with at the moment. But it is a strange comfort to see the power of the internet. If Magnus is truly keeping her somewhere in this realm, we might have a real chance at finding her with this method, as off-putting as I find it.

"You're just going to keep pacing all night, aren't you?" Marsha asks, and I did not realize I had begun again.

"It is likely," I answer honestly.

Sprout picks up his head, letting out an annoyed huff.

"Am I disturbing you?" I ask, dipping down to pat the fur of his head. The large hound picks himself up and walks to the bedroom, claiming the center of the bed with a flop.

At least one of us will be getting some sleep tonight.

"Come on," Marsha says, patting the empty spot on the couch. "Heather has got to have a *Gilmore Girls* DVD or something around here…"

Heather

"Here I thought I had been keeping a princess in the tower..."

"Oh!" With all the dissociation I hadn't heard Magnus come in. When I fully come to my senses, I realize I'm half-shifted again. In the mirror, I catch a glimpse of my milky green eyes and claws that have torn the fine silk sheets strewn around the bed.

Great.

"Get you a girl who can do both," I groan, wrapping the blush pink dressing gown tightly around my body. Earlier, I stumbled back up to the tower after realizing it was too weird to remain in the vampire king's bed. I know it's only been a few hours since, but after the haze of sleep, my body craves a cup of morning coffee. "Did you want something?"

"I believe you requested a date in the mortal realm." He crosses the room and pulls the chair from the vanity, so that he can sit across from me where I'm reclined on the bed. "Forgive me for saying so, but you seem to need a little more time to get ready."

"Right." I roll my eyes. I'm not nearly as shifted as before—just a few feathers and the opalescent eyes—but for the mortal realm, yeah, it's probably a little much.

I close my eyes, breathing in.

"Holding my hand seemed to help last time," he says, trying to put his hand in mine. "If you'd like, I could—"

"It's because I was thinking about *him*," I interrupt, clasping my hands together. I fight the urge to apologize but can't bring myself to do it. Moth would help me make sense of all of this. He'd call me beautiful, he'd—

"Ah, it makes sense, thinking of the prince would help you change back to the form he knows and loves," he says. "You really are remarkably beautiful."

"If this is the part where you do an evil monologue telling me that Moth doesn't love me anymore or something, save it," I snap, stepping behind the dressing screen and slipping out of my dressing gown. Considering the wardrobe for a moment, I select a more modern baby blue shift dress with dramatic puffed sleeves that hits above my knees. "He does. You suck. The end."

"A lovely start to the evening," he says, offering his arm. "Shall we finish this?"

"Absolutely."

My plan was to get Magnus to take me to the diner near the cabin. Unfortunately, even with how out of touch he is, he does in fact know what a low-budget diner is and insists that, if the date in the fae realm was too much, this would be too little. I hate to admit that he might be right. Sheer desperation may be clouding his judgment, but he knows I'm plotting something by wanting to come back home. Which is why we've been seated silently since our server brought water and a menu.

"Squirrels." He says the word so softly I'm sure I must have heard him incorrectly. I mean, yeah, we're on a balcony but I don't see any trees—much less squirrels.

"What?"

"You asked what kinds of things I like."

"When I was setting up your dating profile?" I ask, and he only nods in response. "And, sorry, your answer is … *squirrels?*"

"Yes."

"I don't hate that." I shrug, making a mental note to add 'fan of squirrels' to his bio as a conversation starter. That is, if I can ever get my phone in working order again. A little bit of quirkiness never hurt anyone. Who knows, maybe a hipster with a pet squirrel and a heart of gold will come up on his feed. I swear there was a cute bookstore girl that came across my socials ages ago that had the exact same—

"Heather?"

"Yup, sorry, just mentally matchmaking."

"I wish you wouldn't."

"Why?"

"Because it's something I should have never agreed to." He looks off, his mouth slightly open as if he's debating on saying something. He clamps it shut with a shake of his head. Finally, he takes a piece of paper out of his pocket; it's creased and messy with splotches of ink.

Magnus – 25 – Male – Leo
A Vampire King looking for a queen.
Has a fondness for the Hurdy Gurdy, a strong cup of almond tea, and squirrels.

"A start, as you said—*something honest.*" He looks bashful. "If I manage to get another cellular device, I will continue to workshop it. Though, I still do not know what to look for."

"Then answer that question I asked you in the Dragonfly Court," I say, taking a sip of my drink and hoping I can maybe get a real answer from him for once.

"Which one?"

"Describe your dream partner to me." I say it with the seriousness of a quiz in a teen magazine, but he exhales, thinking for a long moment before his mask slips back in place.

"Why would I bother when I'm sure I'm staring her in the face?" Magnus has that same sly smile, but there's something in it that doesn't reach his eyes this time. We're both so tired.

"Humor me here," I press.

"Fine. Beautiful, good sense of humor, not afraid to stand up for her morals—someone who would fight for me." Maybe, just maybe, we're starting to get somewhere.

"See, that's how you know we're mismatched." I shake my head.

"Hmm?" Magnus murmurs, his eyes fully locked on mine.

"All I want to do is fight *with you*," I reply. Somehow, at that, we both laugh.

"Perhaps I am looking for a bit of that as well." He runs his fingers through the length of his red hair. "Someone to keep me in check—someone like you. That would be enough."

I look at him seriously. "But don't you think you deserve more than just enough? Magnus, you should want everything."

"I have you."

"You don't. And even if you did," I sigh, resting my head in my hands, "it would never be reciprocated."

He bites his bottom lip, his fangs worrying the skin. "What is it about him that's so different? Tell me, why does that brute get to be your 'everything' when I am right here?"

"The whole 'I love him' thing is a big one."

"Yes, but why?" He says, fully exasperated. "Why him and not me?"

"He sees all of me." I sigh. "The good, the bad, hell… the really bad. I act before I think. I trust *so* easily, and it gets me into trouble. Case in point: my present company."

He raises his glass in a cheer, and God, I resist the urge to push him off the balcony and into the street. Let's appeal to his better sense—assuming he has them at all.

"All of that and he still loves me. Plus, he makes me feel safe—physically and emotionally. I can just *be* with him. I don't think I've ever felt that with anyone else."

"He makes you feel all of that?" he asks, his gaze suddenly fixed on the bubbles rising from the sparkling water he ordered.

"And more." My heart aches just thinking about him.

"And one of those potential suitors from your broken cellular device could do the same for me?"

"It's worth a shot, isn't it?" I ask. "Especially if you find something that's mutual."

His eyes glitter for a moment as if thinking about the possibilities. "Then … if I was to find someone, we could go on a double date instead of a fake one." God, it would be cute if it wasn't so short sighted.

"Oh, Moth is still absolutely going to kill you," I say, and even though it's probably an exaggeration, Magnus isn't coming out of this unscathed.

"Not if he can't find us."

"Then how exactly are we going to do this emotionally mature double date?"

"You will have to sort out the details of having me spared of his rage." He smirks.

"You're ridiculous."

"You could feed my ego every once in a while, you know," he grumbles. "As wonderful as it sounds to be truly seen, I would not mind a compliment."

"Then we'd better find someone else." *Preferably someone who doesn't mind a few dozen red flags.*

The server brings our order, and while it's less impressive than the beautiful spread from the restaurant in the Dragonfly Court, it's allergen-friendly and the portions are huge. Considering I've been eating like a bird the past few days, I dive in.

"How is my performance this evening?" he asks, an earnestness to his voice as he leans in. "If I were to date a mortal, would I do well?"

"Yeah, totally," I say between bites because, honestly, I'm too exhausted and hungry to give him any more attention—and this is the most pleasant night we've had together. He beams regardless, and I watch him bite into the appetizer I ordered for us to share. As much as I'm enjoying the honesty, I'm hoping the roasted garlic hummus gives me the upper hand in whatever happens next. Though, I'm still not totally sure of the rules on all this vampire stuff.

"Why did you decide to do it?" I ask. "Like, I understand you thought you were going to save me from a life of misery or whatever, but why? You learned everything from my clothing size to my dietary restrictions. You were lonely. I get it. We met and I was cool and interesting and—"

"Stunning."

"Okay, yeah." Flair up or not, I did look incredible that night at the ball. "But what I was going to say was, I was new—"

"That wasn't it," he says, cutting me off. "You helped me—I thought that meant you wanted to be together."

"People just help sometimes…"

"I haven't found that to be true in anyone—apart from you and Gil," he says bitterly, his fingers tapping along the table before he stills them around his water glass.

"Then maybe you need more experience." I cringe, expecting him to reply with something gross and flirty.

Instead, he hums thoughtfully to himself and nods in agreement. The silence that stretches between us is not comfortable, but not exactly awkward either. I eat my food and watch the human couples walk by, holding hands and giggling to each other. Some are obviously on first dates, and others seem like they've been together for years.

"We are not going to fall in love, are we?" Magnus's voice finally breaks the silence.

"Not in a million years."

"A 'no' would have sufficed."

"Honestly, I don't think I could be clearer in this situation," I say, and despite all of this, I laugh.

"Then," he says, rising from his seat, "the party tomorrow will be our last together. After that, I will say the words."

"You're serious?" I shake my head. "Why not break the deal right now?"

"The selfish desire for your company one more night—plus, couldn't you annoy the court just a little more for good measure? I want to assure that you're not missed."

"Fine," I agree, knowing I shouldn't. "But you know you owe me, right?"

"I will be in your debt for an eternity," he says, his lips spread in a genuine smile. The terrible thing is … I believe him.

18.

Moth

OST OF OUR RESCUE PARTY HAS relocated to the cabin to watch the slew of comments from Marsha's cellphone. We tried to convince her to come with us to the castle, but she was firm that she did not "pack any castle outfits" and I was too tired to argue. My flame may be different from her mother, but in some small ways, the apple has not fallen far from the tree.

The tagged photographs are blurry and clearly not Heather, but it has gotten traction which Marsha assures me is a good start. Oak and Clara chat easily with my mother-in-law about things like photography and the internet which I do not understand, while Pepper sharpens weapons that I hope we will not need. It is a full house, though Mother, Holly, and Ruby have remained in Eclipsica. It seems I have become the unwilling host of a disgruntled party—a party that, from the sounds of it, has another guest.

Hurried footsteps rush to the doorway, accompanied by the sound of something being dropped as if we've received a delivery, which is odd considering our postal box is at the end of the road. Sprout picks up his head before a loud knock reverberates through the cabin, and I wonder who has joined us this time.

Moving to the door, I open it to see a strange assortment of items that are lined up on our welcome mat. Namely, pepperoni rolls and a bottle of green off-brand soda. Strange… similar offerings have been left at my statue in Point Pleasant over the years. They are favored by the locals—including me during my many years in their woods—and it would be a lie to say the familiar scent does not tempt me…

"Don't freak out!" Chris—the sorry excuse for a hunter—stands a comical distance away from the house. "I'm here to help!"

What kind of help could he possibly offer?

Before I can bear my claws, Rosie leaps into action, racing down the porch steps and toward her brother.

"No! Nope! Absolutely not!" She punches the man in the chest with every new word to punctuate her point. "Why. The. Hell. Do. You. Keep. Showing. Up. Here?" While he flinches, it is not nearly enough pain…

But it is a start.

"Did you do something to her?!" she screams, continuing to pummel her brother. And something in me snaps—his involvement in this situation was not something I had previously considered. The thought of this man palling around with Magnus is enough to make my stomach lurch. But I must stay focused.

"Holy shit." He throws his hands up in the air. "Stop, *stop!* Please, just listen. I promise I'm not here to cause problems."

The fool has backed toward me, and Rosie clears the way so I may move forward. Baring my teeth, I shift into the monster he feared and hunted two years ago. My claws flex. I will not kill this man, *but he does not need to know that.*

"Wait! I'm here to help!" he begs. *Hm, doubtful,* but I do enjoy the way he is cowering. "Please, man, hear me out. I promise I wouldn't have come back without a good reason."

"Explain yourself." My claws twitch, itching to be done with this. I will never tolerate this disgrace of a mortal darkening our doorstep again. Rage boils within me at the thought of what men like Chris and Magnus have done with their unwanted obsession. How dare they have caused my flame such pain and distress.

"I think Heather is in some kind of trouble—she is, isn't she?" He frantically glances toward my future mother-in-law as if she will save him or at least help mediate. Considering Marsha is now armed with the knowledge that this man shot her daughter, she does not budge.

The growl I emit is guttural, and I find my resolve fading. Perhaps I will maim him ever-so-slightly for the crime of allowing her name to pass his lips.

The group has now gathered outside to watch the show. Oak mutters something about making popcorn, while Pepper stands ready with a blade. But this infernal mortal persists.

"Why should I not kill you where you stand?"

"Because," Chris says, backing away. I follow each step, keeping my eyes trained on him. "I think I know where she is…"

He—*what?*

There is a flash of light below us in the trees—a portal has opened. My sister tumbles through, a mess of blue wings and periwinkle hair, before she straightens, brushing leaves off of her clothes.

"Compatriots!!" Holly springs toward us, her gaze focused on me, not the surrounding chaos. "Promising news! Gil has made much progress on the wards and—"

"What the fuck?" The human hunter gawks. Concurrently, my mother-in-law's jaw goes slack. I sigh. At least now she can see an example of the portal travel we described yesterday.

"This is Chris. He's Rosie's—" Clara begins and within seconds, Holly's blade is at the man's throat. A fair reaction, one that I am unsure I want to put a stop to. This man will not die by my hands. I cannot make the same promise for my sister.

"Oh, I know *exactly* who you are." She narrows her eyes, looking at him like he is a rat who has clawed its way into our home. She is wrong, of course, a rodent would be welcome. "And I should skin you alive for what you've done to Heather."

Tension hangs thickly in the air.

"Yeah, we got past the overt threats of violence about two minutes ago," Rosie says with a glance at her watch.

Holly raises her eyes to me, and I nod, confirming what Rosie said to be true. At that my sister withdraws, heaving him away from her person like a bag of garbage being tossed in a bin.

"It is just as well." She crosses her arms and shrugs. "This is a new gown, and his blood seems unworthy to stain it." I let my fangs spread into a smile.

"Oh my God," Chris wheezes, his eyes wide. It would be so easy to snap him in half. And I doubt the god he calls to would save him.

"The information. *Now.*" It is bad enough to speak to him—to know that he has knowledge about Heather's whereabouts that I could not find makes me feel that I have failed. But, I will not let my pride keep me from what could be valuable information.

"Yes! Okay, look, it's right here. Look." He pulls out his phone and shows me a website that reads 'CRYPTID SIGHTINGS' in a bright green text. "There's this forum I go on, and one of the subjects is this guy with the red hair. There's something about him that's eerie, right? Anyways, I'm scrolling and all of a sudden, I see this—" With the flick of his thumb, the screen moves, revealing a series of photographs.

At first, they appear to be King Magnus through time. But I do not believe that's true… The first man has hair far too light, the second a forehead too wide, none of them are consistent. Though they are similar and perhaps related, I do not believe them to be him.

"Everyone says he might be a vampire," Chris says with an expression that reminds me of a dog bringing home a bone and expecting a treat.

"That is not new information," I say flatly.

"Chris, you promised you'd stop going on those monster hunter forums!" Rosie says. A deep frown creases her brow, and I wonder if she thought he was capable of keeping such a promise.

"I know, I know. It's just… I've been talking to the old group again, the guys from high school, and they've got such a different outlook on things. I've been—"

"Skip to the point," Clara snaps, crossing her arms as she takes a step in front of Rosie. I would venture to guess that there has been more stress and strained communication between them that I am not privy to, nor would I expect to be.

He is Rosie's family by blood—and though it has been a complication for my flame and me, I can imagine it has been stressful for the humans. Seeing them together now only confirms it. The betrayal and hurt is so thick in the air you can almost taste it, though he seems oblivious. Perhaps he has been micro-dosing their disappointment for so many years it fails to affect him.

When he hesitates, I stand at full height. It is only a little satisfying to see the way he squirms in discomfort. He reaches for, then drops, and reaches for his phone again. Despite the strangeness of his peace offering, I am glad he has not forgotten I am something to be feared. With shaking hands, he shows me the next series of photos.

Long chestnut hair and freckled skin—it is her, on the balcony of a restaurant. From the style of the building, it appears to be somewhere in the mortal realm. The vampire king is at her side, but more chilling than his presence is the smile that adorns her lips. They are laughing, blurred in motion, and there's a look on her face I thought was meant for only me.

"And you know where this is?" I ask through gritted teeth, resisting the urge to turn the cellphone to dust. I know, from experience, they crumble quite easily.

"Yes! I'll go with you," he offers. I laugh. He has to be joking if he thinks I would allow such an action.

"No," I say, shaking my head. The mere thought of having his joke of a human near any of my dearest friends makes my claws lengthen.

"Come on, I promise I can do this—" he begins, attempting to cross into the threshold of the cabin. With a small pivot of my body, he is easily blocked.

"You will not step into our home," I say, standing firm.

"Okay, fair. I can wait at The General Store. Call me in for backup. "

Rosie shakes her head. "I promised Heather you're still banned there."

"But she's not—" I glare, and the hunter presses his mouth shut. "So, the farm?"

"I don't really want him at our house either," Clara whispers to Rosie under her breath. I can tell from the way Clara nervously fiddles with the strands of her teal hair, there is no love left between them as family, married-in or otherwise.

"Okay, so I'll just stand outside wherever you all are meeting and—"

"You are not, and you will not, be a part of this," I say with a finality I hope is hard to argue with.

"I hurt her once. Let me try to save her," Chris begs, his eyes glassy and tinted with remorse. He is sorry, that much is certain, but it does not change the fact he must go.

"Imagine on the day of her rescue, Heather sees your face, how do you believe she would feel?"

"She'd…" Chris begins, his smile wavering into a deep frown. "She'd hate it, wouldn't she?"

"If you are truly sorry. If you truly want to do right by Heather, as you have said, you would have sent a message to your sister instead of showing up here. You will always want her forgiveness. It is her right to never give it to you, understand?" I say. "You should not have come."

"I will do anything," he says in his sad earnest way, and I know it to be true. I could ask him to charge into King

Magnus's castle with nothing more than a wooden sword and he would agree—but he will *never* be a hero in this story.

"Then heed my flame's wishes—and do not return," I demand. "She will not give you redemption, but you may grant her peace."

"Okay." He gives a hard swallow before finally accepting my words. "I am sorry—for everything."

"And that matters very little," I respond, not caring that it is cold. The foolish hunter retreats into his car, leaving the information in Rosie's hands, and I am pleased it has fallen to a source we can rely on. We have the threads from the "forum," as Chris called it. The website seems to update with new theories by the minute, and though most of it is focused on Magnus, we have a location.

"We should organize," I say, once the chaos has settled. Too many of us are gathered in one place, and we should split our resources. "I will go in search of Heather, along with Holly and we could use Pepper's skills if this turns out to be some kind of trap. Mother will remain in Eclipsica, waiting for word. Marsha, you will stay at the cabin with Clara in case Heather makes her way here. Oak, you can—"

Oak stands from his place on the porch and stretches his wings. "I will take on my duties as Uncle Oak with the children—Gods know Ruby will need reinforcements with her little cherubs by now."

"And I'm coming with you," Rosie says to me. "You need someone who knows how to work a phone in case more information comes in."

"Then let us go." If Heather is truly on this mortal plane, we have no time to waste.

19.

Heather

THE VAMPIRE'S DOMAIN IS CERTAINLY ... *spooky*. Though I haven't seen anything outside the castle, the shadows surrounding us tonight are a dark mist. There's a smell of dampness in the air, so different from the fresh florals that waft down the hallways of Queen Plume's castle. Standing on the landing, I reach out to touch the banister and a thick coating of dust cakes my fingertips. Either no one has been here in a long time, or they're forsaking cleanliness for the sake of aesthetic.

I was so angry the last time we ate in the dining room, I barely paid attention to any of these *charming* details. Maybe if I would have looked around more while trying to set Magnus up, I would have leaned into finding him a nice goth girl to settle down with, but we're past the point of doing each other favors.

Magnus leads on with no apologies for the state of things, which leads me to believe he must be used to this. I get the whole spooky haunted castle vibe, but there's theming but he probably has enough money to invest in a Roomba.

I wipe the dust off on a fold of my dress and take in the sight of an equally disheveled landing. Despite its worn appearance, there's a warm glowing light flickering down the hallway, accompanied by music and the clinking of cutlery. Each step forward feels like I'm walking toward a haunting—not a celebration.

"Don't worry," Magnus assures me by placing a hand on my shoulder. "It is a less favorable group than last, but I'm sure they will hate you just as much as you intend."

"By 'less favorable' do you mean stabby?" I ask. "Or are they just going to make fun of my outfit behind my back?"

"With me on your arm, they wouldn't dare." The answer doesn't give me the clarity I was hoping for. Reaching into the pocket of his red velvet jacket, he produces a small key-chain, part of it at least.

"Oh my God!" I squeal, jumping up to snatch the ridic-ulous thing from him and hold it tight to my chest. Moth will totally laugh when I tell him how much of a silly com-fort this thing was while I was gone, but damn, I'm glad to have it back—even if it's still snapped in half.

"It was found on a staircase; I couldn't have thought of anyone else it might belong to." He laughs, shaking his head. "You really do love him, don't you?"

"With everything I have."

He sighs, offering me his arm. Against my better judg-ment, I take it, allowing him to lead me into my last night in the vampire's domain.

"Now," he straightens himself as we reach the doorway, "time to break our fake engagement, I suppose."

"Why is this dinner so important to you anyway?" I ask. The last one seemed like a nonevent, and I don't think anyone in his court will be sad to see me go.

"Ah—" Magnus flushes a little. "This was meant to be our wedding rehearsal."

It has been another uneventful, albeit fancy, dinner with annoying nobles. I'm grateful—but startled—when the cellphone I hid using a garter on my thigh begins to vibrate. Magnus figured the thing was too water-logged after falling into the spring at Gil's, and honestly, so did I. But when I asked him to bring me two cups of dry rice as a snack after we returned to the castle, he didn't question my human diet. And though it's been glitchy at best, it is kind of … almost working. As the phone sends another round of vibration up my leg, I jump, and all eyes drift toward Magnus and me. Someone smirks knowingly as if they've discovered us in the midst of an act of voyeurism and—

Ew, as if.

"Will you excuse me for just a moment?" I ask, and no one objects this time. If anything, I think I hear a sigh of relief from the far side of the table.

I've continued to be as annoying as possible, now more to soften the blow of our breakup than anything else—and it's absolutely working. Magnus trusts me now. We're almost done with this weird week, and strangely enough, I kind of like him—after our dinner together last night, at least. Something about the honesty, banter, and the way we joked made me feel like, in another life, I think we'd be friends. However, today is the last day of him as my kidnapper, and I'm not going to risk losing my chance at communicating with the outside world just because I'm warming up to him.

Slipping away, I head toward the corridor, in search of a few bars of cell service—because obviously I can't take the call in the dining room, and I don't want to head all the way back up to the tower. The phone continues to vibrate as I head down the hall, concealing myself behind a large staircase. The screen isn't showing a preview and, with the persistence of the caller, it's either Moth or someone calling about my car's extended warranty.

"Babe!" I quietly squeal into the phone, assuming it's him. "Oh my god, I have so much to tell you."

"Where are you?" I guess it makes sense that we don't have time for pleasantries. "I am in the *pshhhhhh* looking *shhhhh—*"

"You're breaking up."

"We are *what?*" His voice is panicked, and I can only imagine what he heard.

"No, oh my God!" I practically scream into the phone, holding it for dear life. "*The call!* The call is breaking up!"

"*pshhh pshhh* mortal realm—restaurant."

"I'll be back tonight! Magnus said he's breaking the deal between us."

"*Pshhhhhh shhhh.*" The static overtakes whatever he's trying to say—and damnit, can't we just get one more minute?

"Babe. Babe? The call is not working. I love you, okay? I love you—love, love you. I'll be back tonight. I promise," I say into the phone, wondering if I should risk hanging up and dialing him again.

"What are you doing?" Magnus suddenly asks from the doorway. The phone falls from my hands. "Is that—" His mouth creases into a frown.

"Oh Heather…" He strides forward, picking up the stolen phone. "You didn't need to hide this from me. Did you speak to your lover?"

"Yeah, the signal was choppy, but I was able to tell him you're letting me go," I say. "And thanks, with everything that's gone on, I was sure you'd be pissed."

"I hope he is pleased you will be home soon, though I will be devastated to see you go." There's the same teasing tone as always, the smug smile. "You know, I was thinking…"

"*What?*" I ask, taking a step back. None of his thoughts or plans have meant good news for me so far.

"Why bother making a show of our breakup? Perhaps you could humor me with just one little run-through of what our nuptials would look like?" He reaches to cup his hand in mine but falls short, letting his fingers brush past mine as if I'm a ghost.

Somehow the pair of us have begun to walk, as the conversation turns into something I hope won't become an argument. We pass the dining room, Magnus keeping his voice low all the while walking me down the long hallway to his quarters.

"Furthermore…" he says with a frantic energy I don't like, as we enter his room—presumably so we can speak more privately, "seeing as you and your lover now reside in the mortal realm, consider this! We get married and fake your death. I will be in deep mourning as far as the court is concerned and—"

No.

No, no, no, no, no.

"You're just going to keep doing this, aren't you?" I gasp, stepping away. I've once again let my guard down. I'd like to blame the bond or Magnus's charm, but *I'm* the problem. Despite discovering a new power within myself, I still just want him to be… well, *good.*

And he's too desperate and lonely to be anything but the bad guy.

He made me feel like I was "someone who finally understood" him, and in some ways, maybe I do.

"Doing what?"

"Are you really going to break the deal tonight? Or are you just going to keep finding reasons to ask me to stay?"

"What in the realms are you talking about?" He has the audacity to look genuinely confused, but it's all a part of the show. The nervous twitch of his lips confirms it. "I am simply offering a way out that suits both of us."

"How exactly does faking my death do that?" I say, and as expected, Magnus does not have an answer.

I thought I was starting to really *get* him—that there was something under the surface I could see myself in. The mask, the fear, the worries about being perfect all the time. But he's not some burnt out influencer like I was…

He's so much worse.

"Is it wrong that, even as just friends, a room feels better with you in it?" he whispers. It should feel like a compliment but, instead, my body wants to stretch and bend and claw. Still, Magnus persists. "If you leave, he will never let me see you again…"

"Stop thinking about what Moth will allow—and think about what I want." I draw in a deep breath, trying to steady myself. I'm my own person; if I wanted to be friends with Magnus, I would find a way to do that while still respecting my relationship…

But how can I want anything to do with a man who wants to keep me in his pocket, the way I do my broken Mothman keychain?

He's right. After this, I'll never see him again. Not because I'm forbidden, but because how could I ever want to? From everything I've seen, his court adores him; he has Gil. I know I've been the closest thing he's had to a new friend in a while but—

"What is it in that room filled with vampires you're so afraid of?" I snap, unable to piece it together, but my thoughts whirl in a frantic mess.

"I am not afraid of them—"

"I told you things." Goosebumps rise across my back and shoulders. "You made me feel—"

Heard in some moments, ignored in others, but I should have known better than to let myself be vulnerable with him when he never intended to release me—not really.

"Perhaps we break this bond and create a new one— bound to visit each other once a year or—" He frowns. "Don't look at me like that. I will let you go; I am just offering *options*."

My claws begin to extend. God, it's getting harder and harder to keep myself together with every lie that passes his lips. The blood in my veins seems to vibrate as it courses through me, like I'm filled to the brim with soda that has been violently shaken.

"Heather, Heather, my sweet. Please." His gasp is sharp, almost pained as he takes a large step backward. "You cannot allow the monster inside you to take shape—not tonight. This is our last night together."

"It might be your last night in general." I focus on the way the tiles of the floor crack just slightly beneath his feet.

"No!" he hisses, his sharp canines on full display. "Everything I said to you last night was true. If I could keep you by my side as a confidant, I would always—"

I stomp, the weight of my leg suddenly heavier than if it was simply clad in a pair of heels. I tense and feel talons—*my talons*—scraping the old stone floor.

"Heather, my sweet Heather—focus, *focus*! Bring your attention back to me," he says, attempting to grab hold of my hands. Magnus draws in a deep breath, slow and deliberate, coaching me to do the same. "Like we did before, count with me or just listen to my voice. One, two—"

Soft needles pierce my skin as feathers sprout one by one, encasing my neck in a wreath, while my eyes swell and harden. The power of transformation is matched measure by measure by the pain coursing through my body. The counting, the soft tone of his voice—instead of calming me, each word drives tension further down my back until I'm all but being ripped apart.

"I am not your *sweet*!" I roar and it feels like fire ripping through my lungs. Footsteps rush into the hall.

Guards? Their movements blur in a display of vampiric powers. I am dimly aware of the tension of my limbs being pulled together by what feels like coarse rope.

"Release her this instant!" Magnus growls, except they don't. The rope winds tighter and tighter until my red vision glosses over like a movie screen, playing footage from the night Chris kidnapped me. I can smell the wood of the barn even in this place of cold stone.

Tied up.

Helpless.

Live bait.

Or in this case, a prize.

No—no! I'm not letting that happen again.

"Do not touch her! Do you hear me?" Magnus's voice rages through the chaos. "By order of your king."

I snarl, shaking off the feeling of Magnus's arms wrapping around me. The only person I want to have and hold is Moth, but that doesn't seem like it stops these men from trying to take ownership of my life.

You'll be happier.

I shrug him off.

I'm doing this for you.

I open my mouth to scream.

Fuck all of that.

I squeeze my eyes shut and open them again, the red cast over my vision is no longer speckled but fully pigmented, like lipstick smeared across a mirror. Everything on the other side is hazy, but I can still see Magnus. He's trying so hard to save me, like a child who's watching their new favorite toy fall into the mud.

Snap.

The ropes fall to the ground.

Crash.

The bodies fall next.

Magnus is among them. He reaches up to touch his face, blood trailing from a split lip. His pretty purple eyes widen, and that lean body shakes as he crawls backward.

"You're—you—" he stammers, backing into a corner. Magnus, the great vampire king, shrinks into someone small and trembling right before my eyes.

"I've been saying this whole time: wait until Moth comes for me. He'll destroy this place. He'll kill you." The shrill sound of my voice bounces off the stone walls, and Magnus cringes, covering his ears. "If you're going to keep me here—I'll do it myself!"

"*Heather!*"

Another rope—this time from behind me—snakes around my body in an attempt to bind my arms to my torso. With a flex of my muscles, it's fallen to the floor along with another set of guards.

"Stop! She just needs to calm down!" Magnus barks.

With a snarl, I dive past Magnus and straight toward the portal he keeps in the corner of his bedroom.

"This isn't you," Magnus pleads, racing in front of me. He holds his arms out wide, blocking me from the portal. "Please, turn back. Forgive me, life was so terribly boring before you came into it. Turn back. Let us talk through this one more time."

"Release me now," I order, straightening myself so I tower over him. If reason won't let him willingly say the words, maybe fear will.

"Do you really think he'll still want you like this!?" he shouts. The tips of my wings bristle at his words. Most of my life has been spent trying to look beautiful. For my mother, for the internet, rarely ever myself. Even on days when my joints ached and I felt pasted together, a good outfit or cute hairstyle had always made me feel … something. But this is more than the confidence you feel when wearing a new pair of heels. There is power here like I've never felt before, coursing through my veins.

My wings spread freely with no consideration for the valuables in the room. I've shifted into this body, and it feels like I've slipped into a new outfit—but I'm still the same person. My joints still ache.

I'm allowed to like both versions, and Moth will too. *Won't he?*

I touch the shape of my face and find a beak where my mouth should be. Panic rises in my chest.

What if I *can't* change back?

Does it matter?

Magnus can't even look at you—what if Moth can't either?

He's different—Moth is different.

"Things don't have to be beautiful to have value," I say, echoing that early conversation. "He's a better man than you are."

"I don't doubt it."

"Then move," I growl.

"I'm not letting you through that portal while you're out for blood. You've made a mess of my court, and I can't risk setting you free now. Besides, you can only travel through them with me, as if I would go anywhere with you."

"Magnus?"

"Yes?" he says, desperately.

"You don't get to tell me what to do anymore." I pick up his body like a rag doll. He's used me this whole damn time; if he's the key to the portal, it's my turn.

"I release you from our bargain," he screams as we crash together into the spiraling void. The last thing I hear before diving through the portal is shattering glass—one more broken mirror to decorate the vampire king's room. Exhaling, I hold tight to a piece of my Mothman keychain in the safety of my tattered dress and think of home.

Moth

NOTHER DEAD END.

The mortal hunter is lucky he did not convince us to let him join our quest. Heather's continued absence would easily make him the subject of my ire. We walk aimlessly in a city I do not know. I can see the balcony they had dined on, and it is clear that they are long gone.

"Ughhh, guys…" Rosie says, staring wide-eyed at the phone.

"I prefer 'companions', 'your majesties,' or 'friends,' if you must," Holly huffs, crossing her arms. It is strange to see her glamoured without wings as we walk through the mortal city. Pepper appears equally strange, and two passersby have already asked if we are "in a band." Even without the frills of our faerie-born appearances, we stand out. Worse, there is no scent of honeycomb soap here—and no sign of Heather. But with the way Rosie looks at her device in horror, I believe she may have a lead.

"You're going to want to see this."

"More rubbish information from your brother?" Holly sighs but snags the phone away regardless. Her eyes widen as her hands clutch the device in her hands.

There are screams echoing from the speakers.

"*What the fuck is that?*"

"*Holy shit.*"

"*Oh my God, oh my God!*"

Screech!

"That isn't—" Pepper gasps.

"That couldn't be," Rosie argues. "No, no, no."

I move to look at the screen and see a creature, a ball of pale green fur and feathers with green and yellow wings spawning from her back—wings I would know anywhere…

"There's more. You know, you have quite a … *fandom*," Rosie says, her voice high-pitched and frantic before she hands me the device. Squinting, I study the details of the footage. My throat bobs at the sight of her exoskeleton. Not only does it act as a protective layer atop the skin, it seems to flow across her curves like a piece of art. I ache to get a closer look.

<*Mrs. Mothman looking for her man?*> The most upvoted comment reads. How right they are. "And it is time I find her," I respond to the comment aloud, as if it is something that has been uttered aloud.

In the blurry video, Heather's eyes snap toward the phone for a moment—owlish and wide—before she launches farther into the sky.

"Play it again," I demand. After Rosie reaches around me to tap the screen, I watch the video with bated breath.

In this new hulking form, Heather deftly navigates the sky, her piercing screech striking fear into all who hear it.

"Take Rosie back to the cabin," I direct Pepper. "Holly, you will follow behind me." The three are clearly in shock, but manage to agree. All the while, I am still transfixed by the image of her playing on the small screen.

There is no denying that it is my flame, and I know exactly where she is.

Racing through the sky, I head back to the place I once ran from—that sighting was near the statue. A strange place indeed, but if it is where the portal led her, then it is where I will go. I wonder if she has the other piece of this keychain—considering she bought the silly thing in Point Pleasant, it would stand to reason it would send her back here…

Though I am thankful my piece sent us back to the cabin, the statue is more than I would like to explain to my sister. When I tracked Heather to their festival of my likeness last year, I had thought they would come for me with weapons drawn and pitchforks sharpened. Instead, there was a fondness I did not think possible—as well as what Heather had called "very anatomically correct" fanart. I only hope my flame will be met with the same enthusiasm if she is encountered.

I fly without rest. Whether it is minutes or hours, I cannot tell. My vision pulses. I fly until the scenery begins to become familiar. This place—the woods, the bunkers— they were my home for such a long time after finding myself in this strange world. I try to remain unseen; the town is quiet today, but curiosity has been stoked by the circulating videos. I dodge more than one curious human holding a camera during my flight.

My vision flicks downward, like an owl hunting for mice in the grass. I see *something*—red shining hair.

King Magnus.

I land and the ground writhes as my talons strike into it. The poor man shakes. He is smaller than I remember. Somehow, in moments of uncertainty, knowing all his efforts were spent wooing my bride, the image of him had become distorted into something unachievable. The wings at his back twitch, a piece of it left looking to have been scratched by claws—and the wound appears to be fresh, as do the marks across his face. Pity they do not seem deep enough.

"Please," he begs. "She's lost control. I'm worried she—"

"*She* is not your concern." The rage I have misused, bottled, and spilled left and right begins to find release. Ruby was right to say I am more than sharp teeth and claws—but now, for her honor and my revenge, I will use them all.

Immortals heal quickly, and while Heather has created what is sure to be a beautiful scar, King Magnus deserves a lesson he will never forget. With a flick of my claws, he screams, clutching his face as blood drips between his fingers.

"You have to listen," the vampire man insists. My flame was correct. He is pathetic. "I will make it right. I will—" His body quakes, curling around itself like a snake hiding among the brambles. If I must look at him for one more second, I may kill him, which Heather explicitly asked me not to do.

Holly lands next to me, wings spread and sword in her hands.

"Would you like to end him, brother?" she asks, offering me the blade while the vampire sputters his apologies.

My flame was right—he really is pathetic.

A shriek sounds in the distance. It is not the sound of prey, but a predator—my predator. My skin heats in anticipation of being found.

"No." I back away, readying myself to launch into the sky. "Something more important than revenge calls."

And it will be my pleasure to answer.

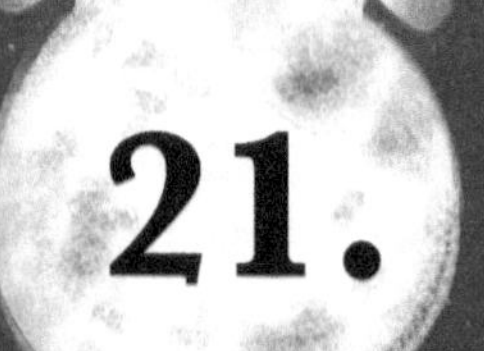

Heather

MOTH FOUND ME.
I should be thrilled—and I am, *I really am*. I want to throw myself into his arms, but I can't let him see me like this. Still, I can't keep myself away either. Diving through the trees, I fight the urge to double back and call his name.

Do you think he would still love you like this?

He would. He will. *He does.*

So why am I running away with his scent on the air? In this form, I can almost taste how close Moth is, and I need him now more than ever.

"My flame!" Moth cries, and I race toward his voice. He's shifted now, his large red eyes even more owlish and wide when they meet mine. When his claws come down to clutch my shoulders, I can do nothing but stare at my future husband.

Do you think he would still love you like this?

"I need you too badly for this game of cat and mouse," he says desperately as we hang in the air, finally together. He's *touching* me, not repulsed, not cowering. Still, I lower myself to the ground and within my wings praying I can turn back.

He fell in love with a human.

I fell in love with a monster.

It's not supposed to be the other way around.

I want to kiss him. I want to throw my arms around him—I want and want and want but my body stays stiff despite the urge to entangle my limbs with his. When I was human, I was worried about not being enough, and now I'm worried I'm too much, I cover my face with my claws. With patience and grace, Moth takes my hands in his.

"Sweet, darling flame—" I feel the weight of his claws easing my own away from my face. "Why would you ever need to hide from me?" His voice is pure midnight echoing through my ears, dropping the tension from my back. His hand gently touches my shoulder and I melt.

"But—"

"You have said you love me in any form. Do you not think I would feel the same?"

I launch myself into his arms.

"How did you even recognize me?" I cry, snuggling my head against the downy feathers of his chest. I inhale the scent of him—somehow, in this form, the scent of autumn is even deeper as I burrow into him.

"My flame," he whispers, "I would know you anywhere."

His beak meets mine in a strange kiss I can't get enough of. For what feels like days on end I have been desperate to feel him, and now we're finally together. It's not the kiss I imagined, but it's everything all the same.

"Moth——" I begin, unsure of what else to say. I love him, God, I love him more than anything. We crumble into each other, warm and content until my feathers melt into bare flesh.

We stand for a long time, his wings wrapped around me, keeping me warm against the cold autumn breeze. I move my hand across his chest and realize my ring finger is missing a very important piece of jewelry.

"My engagement ring!" I gasp, staring at my naked fingers with tears welling in my eyes "It… it must have fallen off when I——Moth, I'm so sorry——"

"It just a piece of jewelry, my flame," Moth coos in my ear, pulling me tight until my head rests against his chest again. "It will be found, or it will be replaced. The most important thing is you are here."

"I'm here. Oh my God, I'm here!" I hug him tighter. Tears I'd been holding in for too long are finally able to fall now that I'm home in his arms. As we start the long walk home, Moth shields me with his wings, though I don't care that every creature in the forest has a view of my body. Neither of us are in any hurry to be anywhere but right here with each other. Eventually, he scoops me up in his arms, and I'm happily carried home.

I pepper kisses on his gold-flecked skin wherever I can reach, but then simply close my eyes and enjoy the ride—the feeling of being back with my forest monster. We catch each other up on what we've missed in the past few days. When I begin to drift off, we launch into the sky, but I'm too tired to keep my eyes open, and finally safe, I fall asleep in his arms.

Home.

This is home.

When I wake up from the deepest sleep I've had in days, it's in our bed, dressed in my favorite pair of pajamas, and the smell of soap on my skin. Vague memories of Moth washing the grime from my body while I was half-asleep give me a warm fuzzy feeling as I realize my knotted hair has been lovingly brushed and sorted into two shiny braids. Sprout lays next to me, and I squeeze his furry body tight and his tail thumps in response.

It's good to be back.

The house hums with activity beyond the bedroom door. Shaking off the sleep, I tentatively open it to see our small living room filled to the brim with, well … *everyone.* Except for Ruby and Pepper who I hope are enjoying a lazy Saturday with their kids. Rosie and Clara are seated at our small table, while Oak, Holly, Mom and even Queen Plume lounge on every other surface available—which honestly isn't many.

"You are awake!" Moth rushes from the kitchen where it appears he was preparing breakfast and takes me in his arms.

"I'm awake and oh my God that smells amazing," I say, my stomach grumbling. "Have you all been here this whole time?"

"I cleared them out upon arrival yesterday. Yet, like rats, they returned come morning." Moth laughs, with no malice in his voice. If anything, he seems *relaxed* in this room filled with people.

"That's a fine thing to say about your rescue team," Oak says, crossing his arms tight across his chest.

"Yeah, we all helped!" Clara says.

"Even some people who won't be mentioned," Rosie grumbles as she and Clara wrap me up in a group hug.

"And you are fine friends indeed." Moth's face softens as he takes in the group that surrounds us. "Truly."

"We were all so worried!"

"I know, I'm sorry." I shake my head, still in disbelief about what's transpired in the last few days. It feels like I haven't been home in years.

"You have nothing to be sorry for," Moth says, firm and reassuring. He gives my hand a squeeze ,and I overdramatically shrug my shoulders.

"*That* depends on who you ask," I counter. "Like you didn't see my whole rampage in the Vampire Court. Oh god, you don't think I actually hurt anyone, right?"

"It was only a little tiny bit of maiming, right?" Rosie says in a small voice. "That's probably okay; he *did* kidnap you."

"Oh my God," I groan, covering my face with my hands. I appreciate how ride-or-die she's being in this situation, but it's taking everything in my power not to jump out of my skin. My wings stay flush against my back as if the act of relaxing even slightly will cause me to transform.

"Heather, from what I saw, you did no more than minor bodily harm. You'd have to practically dismember a vampire to—I'm sorry, is this bothering you?" Holly pauses, noticing the way Clara has pushed away her plate of monkey bread. To be fair, it does look a little too much like intestines coated in cinnamon sugar for comfort.

"Oh no, no, no—we regularly talk about disembowelment at the dinner table," Clara says, her face as white as a sheet.

Wait a second—

"No one was disemboweled!" I shout. "I ... think."

"Dis-mem-ber," Holly repeats slowly. "No one would judge you for tearing a limb or two in your rage."

"Dismem—Honey, we are going to have a long talk," Mom gasps, before wrapping her arms around me. Oh God, I have so much to explain to her.

"Heather will answer to no one," Moth says dryly, a hand on my shoulder and it's oddly just the thing I needed to hear. "And you are not to blame, not for any of this."

"Yeah, we support women's wrongs here!" Clara pipes in. Moth's eyes cut in her direction, but everyone has dissolved into giggles. They all seem to have gotten so much closer while I was gone. I guess that's one thing I can be grateful for.

Holly lets out a sigh, brandishing her weapon.

"No swords in the house, darling!" Queen Plume says, and my mother nods in agreement.

"And Heather, their court was in the wrong for holding you against your will. It is not the days of old. One cannot just steal a bride in the name of anything but theatrics. In my opinion, they still have a boon to pay."

"I will check on the state of affairs," Holly announces, sheathing her sword. She bares her pointed teeth before heading to the place in the living room where a portal glows.

"How? Isn't it still warded?"

"Oh, that was taken care of when I returned the king to his court." She marches toward the portal before pivoting on her heel to face her mother. "I will give you a full report of the chaos. Mother, you should join me, the leaders of both courts are meeting to discuss his fate."

"You go, darling," Queen Plume says adoringly. "You will be queen one day, after all. Have some practice while I get acquainted with Heather's mother." Why do I have the strange feeling these two are about to become BFFs?

Holly beams, clearly delighted by the task, before reaching the portal she doubles back, launching herself into my arms. "I am glad you are back, sister." She says the words in a whisper, holding me close. Tears burn my vision but instead of blinking them away, I let them fall freely.

If anyone is allowed to be an emotional mess right now, it's me. By the time she lets go, I feel exhausted, yet refreshed. I wave her off as she hops a world away.

The room buzzes with questions. I fill them in with what I can and am deservingly mocked for the whole dating profile thing—though, Queen Plume says it was *'crafty'* which I will take. The faeries in our midst clearly feel a level of guilt for not warning me about things like bargains, but I'm just glad to be free from it.

"Can we take a walk?" I ask Moth, reaching out for his hand. He squeezes mine tightly.

"You would prefer that to resting?"

I nod. "I just want a minute with you if that's fine," I whisper.

"It is more than fine." His smile is just the best.

"Oh, hang on," Rosie says, snagging two iced coffees from the fridge. "I was hoping you'd be back soon. I *may* have meal-prepped your fridge while we waited for Moth to get back."

Bless these friends of mine.

Rosemary brown sugar lattes have become one of Rosie's signature items, and each sip I take, combined with the scent of the trees and summer wind on my face, are just the reminder I need that I'm finally home. I've traveled across the vampire's domain all the way to the Dragonfly Court and still, nothing tastes as sweet as home.

Moth's clawed hand interlaces with mine, and the rest of my tension leaves my shoulders.

"This is exactly what I needed." I sigh, swinging our arms in time as we talk.

"You have taken the words from my mouth." Wow, I've missed the way he takes the most casual of sayings and turns them into something dreamy. However, there's a shake to his voice that's unusual.

"When Magnus took me," I begin, and feel the grip on his hand tighten, "he said you wouldn't come for me. He said the way I left you at the ball made everyone think that I was fickle or something…" My exhaustion is getting the better of my words. I stop, turning so that our eyes meet. "Did you think I left you?" I finally ask.

He shakes his head, then nods, then shakes his head again. "It would be a lie to say I had no moments of uncertainty," he says. "Then there was a picture of you on a … *date* with him."

"Ew gross! It wasn't a real date."

"I do not doubt it." He hangs his head, the red of his eyes shining with a sad gleam. To think this beautiful, strong creature could care so much for me that he would worry I'd find someone else. "Your scheme with him was … interesting."

That's a word for it. He should know I'm not interested in an enemies to lovers romance, not when I have the perfect sweet brooding monster right here in front of me.

"He said he was going to let me go…" I trail off. "Then, when he changed his mind, I just snapped. I'm so sorry for the damage I caused, by the way. I've never lost control like that before."

"It was beautiful," he says, stroking up the length of my jaw and a shiver of pleasure swells in my heart, unlocking a feeling that's hard to describe. At the compliment, my claws grow and feathers spring from the flesh on my arms. My first instinct is to hide it behind my back, but Moth holds my hand steady, placing my palm to his cheek.

"He told me you wouldn't like me in that *other* form," I whisper, "and I know I shouldn't have let it get to me, but it's all just so different."

"The vampire's heart does not know true love."

"No, no it doesn't."

"Nor does he deserve it," Moth huffs, his fingers cupping my chin. "Having you back seems to be the only thing that eases my suffering."

"This is the only place I want to be," I say, fluttering up to meet his lips. He holds me there, pressed against each other in the middle of our woods.

Would he still kiss me like this if I was a monster?

I know the answer—I felt it last night. So why do I want to hear him say the words so badly? Still, right now his lips are soft, quieting my worries. We fit so well together—just like this.

We return home, and it's perfectly cozy. The house is filled with people, trading details and stories. We debate on how to send Gil a last-minute invite to the wedding and wonder what a good thank you gift to a swamp monster would be. Moth seems to be fond of him too, and after hearing more details of his interaction, I look forward to grilling Holly on what exactly happened during the season the Dragonfly Court hosted. Who knew my sister-in-law had so many admirers?

As if on cue, Holly races into the house with a letter in her hand. Evening has fallen and there's a satisfied grin on her face.

"Well done," she says to Moth and me, a proud smile gleaming on her face. God, I must have really fucked shit up for her to be complimenting me like this. She hands me the piece of parchment. "The vampire king seems to have written to you while having his wounds dressed."

"Oooh, read it aloud!" Rosie says, grabbing a seat next to Moth and me on the couch, clearly dying of thirst for one single sip of tea.

Heather,

> *I will not insult you by calling you "darling" or "love"—but I hope one day to be able to earn the title" friend." You are right: as far as romance is concerned, the two of us were not suited. I still search for the "everything" you urged me to find.*

> *While we could never be that for each other, your companionship was more than I could ever deserve. With the apologies of both my horde and the Dragonfly Court, we gift a boon of your choice. Know that we have much in terms of magic and riches to offer.*

> *It is from the bottom of my heart that I apologize for my actions. I should have known better—done better—but, like all who came before me, I was selfish. The scars carved across my face by you and your lover will forever be a reminder that there is more to love than just the selfish wants of this vampire.*

I deserved what was given—if I was in either of your shoes, a stake to the heart would have been a fair option for what I have done. This token will not change our past, but I hope you will accept it and beae no ill will toward the kingdoms I hold an unsteady rule over.

My friendship will remain if you ever choose to claim it.

Kindest Regards,
Magnus

I fold the letter and toss it on the floor. "I told you. Magnus is so pathetic." The room lets out a collective groan.

"And you said I had a flair for the dramatic," Moth grumbles.

"Yeah, he's a lot." I shake my head. "So, you clawed his face up?"

"I merely picked up where you left off." He shrugs. "As he stated in the letter, his actions should have earned him much worse."

"It sucks."

"What does?"

"Is it terrible that I hope he does find happiness—or deserves it, at least?" I frown.

"*Heather!*" The group shouts in unison while Moth lets out a chuckle, his eyebrows furrowed.

"Really though. Even with everything that happened, I don't think he's all bad. Misguided, terrible priorities, sure, but he was so, so lonely."

"So, send him a barn cat, not an olive branch," Clara huffs.

That's not a terrible idea. Magnus does seem to be a cat person and it would be more practical than… what did he say his favorite animal was? A hedgehog, maybe? I don't remember, and it doesn't matter, but the point is: he did seem to like cute, fluffy things. He'd protect it—and it would destroy the hell out of his castle.

"Your heart is too big for your own good," Moth says, calming the chaos of our friends' voices. I nod. That's a pretty diplomatic response considering everything that's happened. "He can have his happiness, so long as it is far away from you."

"You are not the only one who has made questionable choices," Moth huffs. "I hope you can forgive me for accepting information from the hunter."

I shake my head. He explained it all when we walked last night; we had so much to catch up on, and even in my exhausted state, I'm just happy he kept looking for me.

"There's nothing to forgive." I shake my head, looking from him, to Rosie, then Clara. "Thank you for having my back… all of you."

Chris wanted to hurt Moth—and he didn't care if he hurt me in the process.

Magnus never wanted to hurt anyone, despite how selfish and messed up he was for holding me captive. *Why am I defending him again?*

"I know it's probably not fair, considering what I said about Magnus, but you were right. When it comes to Chris, I just—" *I never want to see him again.*

And I'm glad Moth and my friends know me well enough to support that.

I can't even bring myself to finish the sentence. Moth takes my hand in his, placing our hands on top of my chest.

The warm feeling of his flesh encompasses mine makes my heartbeat steady. I exhale.

"Heather, he's my *brother* and this still hasn't wiped the slate clean," Rosie says. "He's grown though, and that's something I didn't count on. I might let him sit on the porch at Thanksgiving this year."

"Maybe in the middle of the yard, if he's lucky," Clara jokes.

Moth brings me back with a squeeze to my knee.

"Just because you have a big heart doesn't mean you need to allow everyone inside," he says, and the feeling of his fingers across my skin is just as much a comfort as his words. He can meet me right at my most flawed and forgiving (or unforgiving) and accept everything he sees.

"You know it's yours, don't you?"

"And I am lucky to have it." He kisses my hand. "But the next one who tries to steal you away from me will have their skin turned to ribbons."

"Oh, yeah, no. Go for it. I'm so not dealing with any of this again." I shake my head, reviewing kidnapping with the distaste of someone leaving a 1-star review on a local coffee shop. 0 Stars, the Wi-Fi is terrible. "Claw to your heart's content. As long as I'm in your arms, I'm home."

Moth's lips quirk. "You can have everything, my flame," he says. "I will make certain of that." With Moth—there's no doubt.

"Get married already, you two!" Oak shouts, making a face.

"We intend to," Moth says, draping an arm around my shoulder before he pulls me in for a kiss.

After everything that's happened this week, tomorrow is finally the day.

I can't wait.

22.

Moth

SLEEP COMES EASILY WITH THE WARMTH of my flame beside me but does not last. Reaching to feel her body next to mine, I find only blankets and pillows.

She is gone.

Startled, I sit up and race to the door.

Sprout sits on the porch, his tail happily thudding as he nods his head in the direction of the woods. Heather is there, among the trees, her body transformed and beautiful under the soft moonlight. I inch closer to get a better look, but as I approach, her eyes widen, pulling her human features back over herself like a security blanket.

"Wait!" I order, stroking her feathers just before they vanish. *Soft.*

Even in this form, she is still *so soft.*

"It's weird for you though, isn't it?" she asks, still half-shifted. "I know how you're used to seeing me."

"You are beautiful."

"Beautiful," she echoes. "I knew you would accept me but… you really think I'm beautiful?"

I cannot help but smile. Perhaps now she understands the confusion I felt the first time she kissed me while transformed. It is not a form mortals are accustomed to, but she is no longer a mortal—and every inch of her is mine.

"What was it you said to me all those years ago now?" I muse, still holding onto her hand. I raise it from where it had rested over my heart to my lips. "'You are so, *so* pretty.'"

"I really am a wordsmith, huh?" She sniffles, her chestnut eyes dewy. The moon hits the defined curves of her body. Yet in this half-shifted form, she looks so small and uncertain.

"And I *love* you," I say, trailing a claw from her shoulder to chin, a gesture that always makes her shudder. She trembles and leans into me, seeming just a little more relaxed. Her skin returns, and though her warmth is welcome, I am eager to see her full power.

"Does transforming get easier?" she asks. Flexing her hand, the nails grow and retract. "Almost every time it's happened, I've been like so angry that everything becomes a blur…"

I hesitate. I've been able to shift forms since I was a child. It's hard to say if it's something that she will adapt to or not. "I will help you practice."

"Yeah…" She nods. "I mean if you want to. I would like that."

"Heather…" I begin, pinching her chin between my fingers. "Again, I will repeat myself: you are beautiful. I will keep telling you so even if it takes an eternity for you to believe me."

"But do you…" she begins, rocking on her heels. I attempt to study her body language, but cannot imagine how, in a form so exquisite, she could doubt herself.

I have told her she is beautiful, accepted… but with the way she squirms, I don't think she believes it. Unless there is something else she is waiting to hear.

Oh .

"You are desired." The words are an understatement. I could never describe what burns in my chest for her.

Still she blinks at me.

"Yeah?" My flame questions and the doubt on her lips would be maddening if the way they pout was not so adorable.

"Yes." I trail my fingers up the pale flesh of her arms, and feathers sprout in the wake of my touch. As I move to rub her shoulders, I speak the words: "In fur, flesh, and feathers, my need for you is the same."

"And do you need me … *now*?" She is surprisingly bashful in this moment. For a long moment, her eyes are downcast, obscured by long lashes. When her gaze flutters up at me, the chestnut color has been replaced with something pearlescent.

"Always."

I watch her come alive under my gaze. My throat bobs as she moves from my grasp, sauntering backward, her body beautiful and bare under the glow of the moon.

I am glad we sent her mother to stay at Rosie and Clara's. An interruption would not be welcome in this—or any—intimate moment between us.

"Prove it." She takes another step back. No, as much as I would love to show her my desire, after all the time spent wondering and chasing her across the realms, I long to feel the same … *dedication.*

"No, my flame," I say, summoning the kind of wicked grin I know will capture her interest. My wings unfurl behind me. "Tonight, I have a request…"

"*Oh?*" Her eyes grow wide with interest. "Tell me."

"You will be the one to lead the chase," I say, straightening my back. Her eyes burn into mine as heat rushes to her face. "Use your strength, claws, and mouth to mark me as your own—if you are willing, of course."

Her eyes grow as wide as saucers, and I wonder if the request is too much for tonight. I will gladly wait—then I note the way she bites her bottom lip.

She is just as hungry as I am.

"That… that sounds. Yes. Yes, let's do that." She nods and her laugh lights up the forest. "Okay, okay, any requests or boundaries we need to flesh out first?"

I shake my head. "All I want is to be caught and claimed by the creature I love most."

"Then Moth?" she says, stretching her arms over her head and shifting her weight from side to side as if she's about to run a marathon.

"Yes, my flame?" I gulp as something *primal* awakens in me.

"*Run,*" she says, standing firm and powerful. It is an order I do not hesitate to follow.

Launching into the air, I fly at full speed. To catch me, she'll *have* to transform, and my body tingles in anticipation of seeing her like *that* again. From flickering flame to screeching monster, she is mine to love in all forms.

And I do—usually Heather is warm against the cool of my feathers. I have often admired the way her freckles pop when she's been exposed to too much sun and that funny way she squints when she laughs. As I soar above the trees, I think of the woman chasing me, I would not change one ounce of her humanity.

There have been times she has asked If I might love her a little less if we had met in a different time. I would not. I *could* not. If she had been a faerie in the Moth Court when I was still indebted to royal life, we would be seated together on the throne. But chasing each other down in these woods—her teeth on the base of my throat and breath on my lips—is the place we belong.

And with every wingbeat, I long to feel all those things and more, but each time my little flame gets close I manage to give her the slip. When I look back, she is frustrated— with adorable, narrowed eyes and her hands balled in fists. She lands with a thud, and despite myself I follow. If this is not a game she wishes to play, I will gladly find another.

"Help me," she says, breaking the tension for a moment. I wonder if it is a ploy to get ahead, but I am not used to being in the position of prey, and I fold at her request. She extends her hands, holding mine tight as a smile appears on her lips.

"I thought about holding your hands like this when I shifted back the first time," she admits with a deep breath. When her eyes flick back up to me, they have a milky sheen across them and have grown in size. I try to pull away, but the devious grin on her lips breaks into something that looks *pained*.

"You do not have to shift all the way," I assure her softly. "We have a lifetime to explore each other."

"I *want* to," she says through gritted teeth, getting closer, so close, her form changes and contracts in my grasp, and I wonder if there is anything I can do to help.

"Perhaps if the pain was paired with pleasure." I lightly tug one hand from her grasp. Once free, I trail my claws down her hip. "Then that might ease the burden."

My fingers glide slowly across her flesh. Days have felt like lifetimes, and I will savor every touch. I do not want to rush even a moment of the pleasure tonight promises.

"Moth." She groans as her body tenses under my touch. I allow my fingers to go lower, sliding until they reach the center of her thighs, I lightly caress her entrance, delighting in the way she shutters in response.

Retracting my claw, I dip into her core, circling and pulsing my fingers; the sound of bones cracking accompanies the sound of her moans until my fingers are slick with desire and the panting form of a monster is wrapped around them.

"Magnificent," I marvel, taking in the sight of her strong shoulders and structure. Her exoskeleton begins at her hips, climbing to cover her breasts in a design that fades from gold to green. With her this close, the soft ring of feathers that covers her neck tickle my soft flesh, and I gulp. *Truly magnificent.*

How foolish I had been to suggest running from her.

With the hand she still holds, I guide her to touch my hardened cock as proof that this form is not only gorgeous, but it is her—and that is all I could ever want.

"You are desired, my flame," I say, not breaking my gaze from her pearlescent eyes. I withdraw my fingers from her. "Now, chase me before I lose my resolve and fuck you right here."

In response, her long claws dig deep into my hand, unwilling to let me go. She toys with my cock for a moment, the tip of a blunted claw dragging across the length. I lean into her, moaning into her feathers. *If she keeps me here all night, I will be content.*

"You'll have to get away first," she growls—a challenge. *At full strength I have yet to meet a foe I could not best.* I tug, but her grip is strong. Nothing like the times she has held me down at my request and I have play-struggled under her grasp.

She has me in more ways than one.

I kiss the tip of her beak, dragging my tongue down to her chin in a way that makes her shiver, but still, she does not let go. I smirk, rising to the challenge. *I had thought I'd stay in flesh this evening, but it seems to get away. It seems Heather will not be the only monster flying through the woods tonight.*

There is no pain when my body shifts, only the familiar feeling of hardening limbs as they stretch and lengthen. She's bathed in the red of my eyes. Releasing my hand my flame lunges for my body; it isn't hard to avoid her, but it is amusing to see those bug eyes of hers narrow.

"I'll give you a head start," my fiery monster whispers. "You're going to need it." Harsh and determined. *I like it.*

At her command, I launch into flight, and just as I wanted, she chases me through the sky. Her form is strong and soft all at once and a wonder to behold.

We race, dodging and circling each other, until finally, her talons hook mine, dragging me into flight along with her. Locked tightly in place, we whirl in the sky, free from shame or inhibitions.

"Do you surrender?" she asks, her thighs flush against mine. Her wings flap behind her beautiful and green as the world spinning around us.

"Forever."

The sharpness of her mouth digs into my shoulder. With merciless ease she clamps down, biting as if I am still adorned in flesh and not a creature of shadow and sky. The second time she bites, the screams from my lips sing through the forest—and I do not mind.

Let the whole world know that I am my flame's to take.

With ease, she slams us into a nearby pine; high above the forest floor, the rough of the bark scratches against my now folded wings. But there's pleasure in the momentary discomfort, the way it aches in tandem with the friction of our bodies. I do not mask the whimper that leaves me. If I am to be weak for anyone, let it be for her. Let this woman take my pain, my pleasure, my heart. She will keep it safe, held tight in a place where neither of us hide our desires.

Another bite—this time at my hip, and the bloom of pleasure rises to a peak as she straightens. She grips my wrists, locking my hands over my head.

Our hips are flush, and with each roll of her body, she teases me until I am in blissful agony. When she finally releases my hands, my claws find my way to her hips, holding tight as I position our bodies to meet.

"Desired, my flame," I repeat. "You are desired."

"Show me," she demands, and my bride does not have to ask twice. I kiss every inch of her from heel to beak, letting my hands trail across the hard and soft edges of her body. She quivers under my fingertips, but it's not enough.

With ease, she flips me onto my back, holding me with one arm. My flame dives toward the ground, dropping my body onto the forest floor. She stands above me, her figure illuminated by the moon, rivaling the glow of even the brightest stars. But, she keeps herself just out of reach of my touch, a gleam in her large eyes, as I writhe with wanting just below her. Weak in her presence, I have shifted back to flesh.

She wants proof of my need for her? I am not above begging. Rising to my knees, I shower her in kisses. "Let me have all of you."

I line up my cock with her opening, moving inch by inch into her welcoming body. We match each other movement by movement. She grinds into my hips, her body taking all of me so well. She is warm and tight, then suddenly—gone.

Flipping her head back, she screams—and her angelic face replaces the sweet creature I begged to take me. Every one of her forms is like art.

"I'll need my mouth for what I want to do next," she says, pushing me down by the shoulders with a force that seems to surprise her. And though her lips are soft on my skin, my little flame cannot help but use her teeth, biting down on the flesh of my calf before she moves between my legs.

Her nose slides down the length of my cock teasingly. She moves her face around in what feels like a nuzzle, pulling a gasp from my lips. She begins slowly, but each movement has the power of electricity. Her tongue knows every way to bring me to the cusp of pleasure-, then snatch it away in a cruel little game that keeps me holding tight to the edge.

I am not finished with her yet-—and luckily, my flame seems to feel the same.

Her hot mouth engulfs my cock, skillfully easing me deeper and deeper into her throat, until her nose touches my abdomen. I am at her mercy. I ache to touch her, but she keeps me pinned to the ground, feasting on my body in a way that makes me senseless.

There is no time to regain my composure. As soon as she releases me from her mouth, she is upon me, straddling my hips once more. She grinds against me, teasing and touching with her hands before impaling herself onto my cock. The sudden sensation rocks me toward the edge, ready to explode.

"Hold onto me," she orders. "Transformed." I can do nothing but comply; my bones move easily, throbbing as my length grows inside her warmth. She groans in response, shallowly rocking her hips. I am on the edge of certain bliss as she launches us into the air. Locked in her talons once more, we spin above the canopy of trees.

Under the moon, we cry out together. I feel as if tonight was as sacred as any ceremony; in the forest we are one.

Afterward, we lay together on a nest of fallen leaves, breathing in the air and the scent of each other. "Was that too much?" she asks.

"Never," I say, brushing the tip of her beak just as her feathers give way to soft human flesh. One day, I hope she will know she has the freedom to be too much, too little, too loud, too quiet. As long as she is here—*as long as she is mine.*

"You are perfect, my flame," I say, meeting her chestnut brown eyes. I need her to understand just how much I mean it.

"I love you." She laughs. The feathers on her arms have yet to retract fully into her skin, and she fiddles with them like the loose wool of a sweater.

"Believe me, Heather," I say in earnest. "Or I will chase you through our forest until you do."

"That was my job tonight, remember? Though, you didn't run *that* far."

"How could I?" I ask, letting the feeling of being this wanted wash over me. For days, we have been fighting to get back to each other, and now she is finally here.

"I'm so ridiculously in love with you. You know that, right?"

"Yes," I say, relishing the feeling of her warmth against my skin. "And I love yo—" A yawn escapes my lips.

"As much as I totally love the idea of sleeping under the stars," she begins before trailing off. "Maybe let's move this to the bedroom—beauty rest and all."

"You couldn't possibly be more beautiful," I whisper, letting my claws trail down her jawline.

"Aw, babe—you abbreviated a word," she squeals, hugging my neck.

"I suppose the time spent together has changed us both," I say, trailing my fingers over the edges of her wings. "Is it going to be like this forever?"

"The unpredictable moments of peril or the bliss of our skin on each other's skin?"

"Both, I guess."

"It may be. I cannot predict the challenges we will face in our long lives—but I can say we will be facing them together."

"Then that's all that really matters, isn't it?"

If all of this has taught me anything, it is that I do not wish for our lives to just be next to each other, I want to be fully entangled.

"You're my best friend, I hope you know that." She nuzzles into my shoulder. "I love our lives together. I love all the people in there, but you are my favorite most of all. You're my person."

"I am so glad you fell out of that tree," I say, remembering the way she looked when I first saw her in these woods. Despite not wanting to be discovered, she awakened something in me. I could never have guessed how our relationship would grow.

"And I'm so glad you fell into my heart." She tugs me close until our bodies are flush, and I am tempted to doze right here under the stars. "Forever, Moth."

"Forever, my flame," I say. It is a promise I will keep in all lifetimes.

23.

Heather

THE SUN SHINES IN STREAKS THROUGH our windows, casting a golden hue on Moth as he sleeps. Beyond him, leaves of red and orange press against the window. After sleeping alone in that tower, this is the perfect picture to wake up to. *Moth.* He's so much more than beautiful, and in the still of this moment, all I can do is admire the face of my future husband.

The soft touch of his gold-flecked skin, the way his dark brow relaxes as he sleeps, his freaking adorable antennae bobbling with dreams I hope are as sweet as the wedding cake he's going to eat his body weight in later.

"Good morning," Moth mumbles, his eyes still closed, a ghost of a smile on his lips as if he can feel me looking at him.

"Good morning," I reply, planting a kiss on his lips. "Sleep well?"

"Mmm." He nods, wrapping his arms around me. "How could I not after the night we had together?"

Heat burns my cheeks as I think of the power we shared soaring through the trees. Last night was beyond perfect.

Glancing at the clock, I thank my lucky stars that we still have time for some cuddles. I know the week leading up to a wedding is normally stressful, but I think we set a record for ridiculousness.

"Did Widow make the necessary adjustments to your dress?"

"It's been glamoured for the reveal," I say, booping his nose. "I'm kind of excited. I've always wanted to do two looks."

"It will be quite the costume change," he croons, planting a kiss on the exposed skin of my shoulder before letting out a deep breath. "This feels good."

This.

The smell of the woods, the soft blankets in cotton and linen layered across our bodies, the way his dark curls feel under my fingertips. Yeah, *this*. This is perfect.

The buzzing of my alarm causes us both to groan.

"Why did we decide to do a brunch wedding again?" I whine, pulling myself up from the comfort of our blanket cocoon.

"I believe it was a part of your grand plan for the perfect—"

"Yeah, yeah, you should have talked me out of it," I say, resisting the urge to climb back into bed—and preferably, on top of him.

"Who am I to argue with a Pinterest vision board, my flame?" He smiles, his fangs on full display.

God. I love this man.

The morning passes in the blink of an eye.

Mom's gift to me was unexpected, a private offline photoshoot of Moth and I getting ready for the big day, with the promise that these photos will never grace her social pages. It's nice—for once. I actually believe her.

We sip our tea and coffee while wearing matching lush robes in the morning. Me with rollers in my hair, and Moth with his black curls perfectly messy.

It's not traditional, but then again, neither are we. It's Moth's claws that lace the back of my dress and help me tie the ribbon in my hair. Mom subtly takes pictures, staying out of the way. Moth looks dashing in his suit—something gorgeous that Widow fashioned just for him. It's nice to see him dressed up like this. The color is a soft burgundy, with golden moths embroidered on the cuffs, a blend of fairytale and modern elements that he can't wait to see crumbled on the floor.

Honestly? Same.

I love him in both forms—even if the more human one hates wearing pants.

His Adam's apple bobs as I straighten his cravat. When his ruby eyes meet mine, I've never been so sure of anything in my life: I want to marry this man.

"You ready?" Mom asks, looking from me to her almost-son-in-law. We exchange one more glance, no words need to be spoken. These past few days has felt like a decade, and I can't wait to finally say "I do."

All five of Ruby and Pepper's giggling children flutter down the aisle, sprinkling flowers. It's their first time in the mortal realm, and if the smiles are anything to go off of, I think they're having fun. Sprout walks next, looking dapper in a bow tie my mom made for him. Flower petals cling to his fur, and when he takes his seat next to our youngest guests, we make our entrance—together. With hands joined, we walk slowly down the flower-filled aisle up to where Queen Plume is standing under a homemade arch of fall foliage.

Clara is fully bawling by the time we are standing in front of everyone, and Holly, though she tries to hide it behind the sway of her lace fan, is not faring much better.

Mom takes her seat, continuing to snap a photo here and there before giving me a small smile and stowing away the camera.

This moment is just for us.

"Gathered loved ones." Queen Plume greets the small group of guests with the regality of royalty. I know she had wanted a big affair with the whole kingdom gathered to see our union, but it makes me happy that she accepted not only our wishes but also her role as officiant.

"We are here to celebrate the love between Heather and my son, Moth, Prince of Eclipsica. Usually, a union of this status would be attended by lords and ladies of neighboring courts and a kingdom of subjects—these two would stand and proclaim their love for all to hear as proof of their dedication. But if you know Moth and Heather, you know they have nothing to prove, for the care they show each other day by day is something precious and rare.

We do not gather for this pair to prove themselves. Rather, we are here to celebrate and stand as their community, for not only do they love each other, but we all love them fiercely."

Looking back at our friends, I see the joy reflected in their faces. Gil sits next to Uncle Doug. I hope he has been briefed on all of this. So far, he's either being very cool about the notion of other realms and creatures, or just thinks we really go all out for a theme. As my eyes wander from face to face, I see each family member and friend is misty-eyed. I'm so happy that they're the people we get to share this moment with.

"Whether it is to unravel a devious ploy by vampires, to come for Sunday dinner, or to be an ear when there is trouble, we will always come together for you, my darlings," she says, whispering *'my darlings'* at the end just for our ears only. She pauses to wipe a tear from her eyes before turning to both of us.

"The bride and groom will now exchange words and rings as a symbol of the promise they make on this day."

"Heather—" Moth begins, then clears his throat. His red eyes have an unfamiliar sheen that makes a lump form in my throat. "You are my hearth, my home, my comfort, and above all, you are my inspiration. You have accepted me in the shadows, and I solemnly promise to love and cherish your warmth for the rest of our days."

Sprout comes forward, dropping my ring from his mouth into Moth's hand. And sure, it's covered in drool and definitely has dirt stuck in-between the prongs, but more than anything, I'm just impressed he managed to find it. Moth dusts it off on his suit jacket before placing it on my finger, and I grin.

Now, it's my turn.

"Moth—" I take a deep breath willing myself to get through this without turning into a blabbering mess. "You fell into my life and turned everything upside down. Since then, I've learned about new worlds, met new family, and most importantly, fallen even more in love with you. I love you in the quiet moments, where it's just us. I love you in the chaos of a crowded ballroom and a forest full of trees. It doesn't matter if we're soaring through the sky or walking on the grass, I can feel the way my heart and yours beat together like we were always meant to be standing right here."

I retrieve his ring from my dress pocket and slip the band of golden leaves with black gems onto his finger; not only does it look perfect but it makes things official. Moth is my husband.

To the cheering of our family and friends, our lips meet, and I smile against him, wrapping my arms tightly around my husband.

"My darlings, as beautiful as that was, we have not gotten to the kissing part yet." Queen Plume chuckles. "I believe you have some words to speak?"

"I do," we say in unison, and I burst out laughing. Moth's red eyes crinkle into half-moons, and there is nothing else to say before Moth pulls me in for yet another kiss. Our guests erupt into cheers as Queen Plume tries to regain control of the proceedings.

"By the power vested to me by the crown of Eclipsica and becomeaminister.com, I now welcome you into this new season of your lives. You may kiss ... *again.*"

And we do.

I'm in absolute disbelief that—after the week we've had and all our adventures leading up to this moment— we're finally husband and wife.

"Are you ready?" The sound of Moth's whisper tickers my ear and I nod. We're not just bound together in flesh; we're also bound in feathers.

The sounds of bones cracking meld with the music of the harp, and when Moth and I kiss for the second time, it's not the soft touch of lips, but our beaks that meet.

We walk back down the aisle to more cheering, flower petals, and bubbles. All exit to start this next chapter together; I reach for Moth, and our claws entwine as we launch into our first flight together as newlyweds.

Leaves flutter down from the trees as we fly past, and I laugh, glad to have the extra layers of exoskeleton and feathers protecting my body from the cold. Our clawed hands join as we soar above the trees. I think we'll circle the area and go back home, but Moth leads us further into the woods and seems to have … other plans.

"Close your eyes," Moth instructs, guiding me with a gentle hand. I do as he asks while we slowly descend to the earth. Our feet land on the ground, and the smell of jasmine and pine fills my nose.

Unsure of our surroundings, I hold tight to him, shifting back into my other form. It's freezing. Luckily, my wedding dress snaps right back into place with the magic Widow wove into it.

Opening my eyes, we've happened upon a cottage in the woods. The front is ivy covered, with an archway of flowers similar to the one we were married under.

"Where are we?" I ask because it's beautiful—and strangely familiar, though I can't place where I've seen it before.

Moth leads us toward the cabin; on the door there's a keypad he punches a few numbers into, and the door unlocks.

Did he get us an Airbnb for our honeymoon? Oh my gosh, cute.

When we step inside my stomach flips. Though cramped, I'd convinced myself our little cabin in the woods was perfect, but this place…

High vaulted ceilings allow us to open our wings, and there's a loft at the top with a writing desk. A pile of pillows is in the corner by a large window—and I can just picture Sprout perched in the midst of it.

And the kitchen—God, what a kitchen. Not only is it open with a giant island in the center, it's bright and airy with an herb garden on the windowsill. Wow, this place is a storybook come to life—with room to grow.

"Wow," is all I can say as we walk farther into the cabin. There's something familiar about it, and then it clicks: didn't I bookmark this on Zillow? Whoever bought it must have turned the cabin into a rental property. Perfect timing for our honeymoon.

"Do you like it, my flame?"

"It's perfect," I say, leaning into him. "Maybe too perfect. I don't know if I'm going to want to leave."

"Well, that is rather convenient."

"What do you mean?"

"It's ours."

"You didn't!" I squeal, wrapping my arms tightly around him. I can't believe he did this!

A place to make new memories. Room to stretch our wings, it's everything I've been wanting, but been too scared to ask for.

"Wait, how?" I pause. "How did you buy a whole house?"

"Being the prince from a kingdom in another realm has its perks."

"Why am I picturing you showing up to an open house holding a bag filled with gold?" I laugh.

"That is … not as far from the truth as you would imagine."

Oh my God.

"I realize now perhaps I should have talked to you." He shakes his head. "I do not want you to feel as if you have had no choice."

"Um, I think I can forgive you for buying me my dream house," I say, nuzzling his shoulder. "I can't wait to keep building our life here together."

"Together again at last," he says, pulling me into a kiss. "Now, this is a home."

24.

Moth

IAM RELIEVED THAT MY WEDDING present for Heather was well received. Though the intention I had was to surprise her, I admit the act of keeping such a large secret from my flame caused anxiety to stir within me. What if it was a mistake? The wrong house—the wrong choice? Seeing how happy this has made her eases any tension, but I think in the future such big decisions will be made with her at my side.

As much as I would love to christen our house with the meeting of our bodies–there is a party to return to, and considering we are the guests of honor we do not linger longer than a giddy tour through each room where kisses are exchanged and promises of a future made.

Before long, the pair of us launch into flight to return to the cottage. I am eager to dance with my bride under the autumn sunshine, and by the time of our grand entrance, the party has fully begun.

The brunch bar is set up toward the house where our guests grab assortments of miniature pastries and breakfast items, all prepared to meet Heather's dietary needs. A shame it would be for a bride to not have her fill on the day of her wedding. I grin watching her dance with Widow and Oak while holding a waffle—she may not always be the picture of elegance, and that makes her all the more appealing. She brings a whimsy to my life by not taking things so seriously. Today, apparently, that comes in the form of dancing with breakfast food.

From the edge of the party, I watch our guests mingle with each other. Heather's uncle Doug seems to be adjusting very well to being surrounded by the paranormal, and I pretend to not notice the way Marsha nudges him toward Mother. She is too busy dancing in circles with the children to notice, but I have seen her eyes cast in his direction and when he finally asks her to dance, I do not interrupt. Mother could use a night of merriment without the burden of the crown, and I suppose they would be an interesting match. Rosie and Clara seem off in their own little world; if I remember correctly, Clara loves weddings and I imagine they're reminiscing on their own. For a moment, I wish I had the pleasure of their friendship back then so I might have seen how their affections have grown through the years. I am thankful they are a part of today's celebration and have once again made a perfect playlist.

"I love this song!" Heather's voice carries across the yard, and before I can even register the tune her hands are pulling me toward the center of our makeshift dance floor. Her dress billows with every spin, and when we kiss, I am lost to the bliss of this moment. Our wedding.

A peppy song comes through the speakers, and the small crowd's energy picks up. Ruby and Pepper join the dance floor, and Holly pulls Gil out of his chair in the outskirts to join. Before long our guests are all circling around us in chaotic movements that while dizzying is joyful.

In the decades spent alone, I hardly thought this would be possible, but I have–friends–real ones who showed up when I needed them, a family, and a bride who gazes up at me with more adoration in her eyes than I can comprehend. The impossibility of her alone makes me want to enjoy this all the more–she is mine and I am hers, and I dance with the beautiful woman until our lungs beg for water and our legs ache.

After adequate hydrating, we make our way to the cake–a pretty fruit layered confection decorated in powdered sugar and edible flowers. We feed each other bites by the tip of our claws and share kisses that taste like dessert.

Soon everyone is scattered to tables, eating and sipping coffees and teas–they clink glasses, ordering my flame and I to kiss, and I am happy to meet the request at the slightest sound.

Unlike Heather, I never had a dream wedding. The details of plum and burgundy, menu, and cake were not things that kept me awake and night, though I did what I could to support her vision. Seeing it all come together, however, is yet another reason to not doubt her creative talents. Yet, among the florals, candles, and crafts she is the thing that makes this the best day of my life.

"I love you," she says, looking down at her plate, and for a moment I am unsure if I should be jealous of a confection, but then she takes my hand squeezing it tight, and I smirk at the jam that has stained her cheek. "This is everything I wanted and more."

"I feel the same," I agree, only I am not speaking about the party. Heather is my person, and to celebrate that in front of everyone is a magic I did not expect. She rises, offering me her hand.

"So, then husband, how about the next dance?" she asks, and the words are sweeter than any slice of cake.

"Nothing would bring me greater joy, my wife."

EPILOGUE

"I'm off to work!" I shout, grabbing my camera bag and heading toward the door. Moth swoops down from the loft, planting a kiss on my forehead before cocooning me in his arms.

His deadline is in exactly one week, and I get the idea he's looking for a reason to procrastinate. I flutter up so that we are face-to-face and breathe in the scent of strong tea as our lips collide.

I guess even faerie-born cryptids depend on caffeine when they're pulling all-nighters. "You did sleep last night, didn't you?"

"I did not."

"Moth—"

"As if my flame cannot relate to a burst of creativity in the midnight hours," he says, tucking the top of my head under his chin. I can feel him yawn. "Yet now, in the morning light, my only desire is to return to our bed and carry you with me."

"I mean, I wouldn't complain," I say, snuggling against him. "Did you finish that chapter you were working on?"

"I fear if I do not answer correctly, I will have to return to my desk…"

"Why?" I tease, my body flush against his. "I love being a distraction."

He growls, pulling me upward. I hook my legs across his waist, allowing myself to be peppered from my lips down to my shoulders with kisses, sharp then soft. We move through the long wallpaper-covered hallways decorated with photos—both candid and staged—of the two of us and the people we love. With each step, he guides us through the living scrapbook of our home until we're back where we started: the large bedroom with a California king bed covered in soft blankets and pillows. I'm happily tossed upon them.

I glance at the clock.

What's being a *little* late anyways? Oak is never on time, and worst-case scenario, Widow will raise her eyebrows at me and start humming some faerie-written love song about "sweet kisses in the morning." I can't tell if she's making it up on the spot to tease me or if it's just a common theme with fae artists. Either way, I can handle a little teasing if it means more of Moth's touch…

We keep it to kissing … and kissing. God, his lips feel so damn good. My body aches for more and my alarm is buzzing for me to get going. But I'm weak to his touch, and it's minutes before we untangle ourselves.

"Okay, now I'm actually off to work," I say, rolling out of the bed and smoothing my dress. "Make sure you eat more than pastries and drink more than tea."

He's a sugar fiend on the worst of days and even more terrible on the days he's sitting at the computer all day.

"I think I have had my fill of sweets—until you return home."

Insatiable, I think as a smile curves at the edge of his lips. We both have busy days ahead, so I make the effort to leave with one last kiss. Our lips lock and I feel his hand at the small of my waist, pulling me close. Inhaling deeply, I break away, comforted by that same woodsy smell of pine and campfire.

"I love you, Moth."

"I love you, my flame." His lips land one more peck before I'm off.

It's not a far commute. Sprout happily bounds through the grass as I make my way to the old shed that we converted into an office. Whoever said you can't have it all obviously never had a cryptid husband and a portal to the faerie realm. Queen Plume wasn't kidding when she said the Dragonfly Court owed us a boon and I was all but happy enough to cash it on this gorgeous magic mirror that serves as my entrance to the studio. We've been open for almost a year now, and Oak was right, the novelty combined with our talents really has made something magical.

I slip into the backroom; from my viewpoint, I can tell the sign is still turned to "closed," which is odd. Until I hear the sound of *moaning.*

Oh my God!

I peer around the corner and find Oak, his arms around Widow whose corset strings are loosened. Oh wow, I should *not* be watching this. They have been flirting non-stop since before the wedding. Widow even caught the bouquet! Now that they're finally lip-locked, I'm so not ruining the moment!

Giggling to myself, I dip back through the portal and slip back into the house. Moth is back to typing, and when he looks up, his face freezes as if buffering. "I was worried you were about to tell me it has been eight hours and I have not gotten down a single word."

"Not quite. I walked in on Oak and Widow *totally* making out," I say, still giddy with the fact they're finally getting together.

"Seems romance is in the air this morning," he says thoughtfully. "I am happy for them—they will make a good match."

"Well." I clear my throat. "Looks like I have a few more minutes to be a distraction."

He licks his lips, a hunger in his eyes burning as if he's just been offered a four coarse meal. I wonder what kind of scene he's been writing.

"I would prefer to think of you as my muse." I shiver at the words. The idea that we can share this idyllic, yet domestic, life together and I still have the power to inspire him is …well, it's more than I could have ever dreamt of.

I hesitate, unsure whether I want to play this coy or outright ask him if he wants help bringing his pages to life. "Well," I say, cracking a smile. "May I *amuse* you?" I decide to take the teasing route. In a lifetime together, there's more than enough time for us to walk both paths.

"Well," he says, fluttering down from the loft, "I could use a proper breakfast." He grins, his mouth filled with fanged teeth. Desire heats me at my core.

But the man has been practically sustaining himself on sugar cubes and pastries since he started this project. For a moment, I'm not sure if the hunger I see in his eyes is for a literal snack—not me. I walk toward the kitchen, which happens to be one of my favorite spaces in our home.

"I think we have some of that vegan bacon from brunch yesterday, but like honestly, sometimes a thing is made from carrots and you can like …. tell." I groan. We need to go grocery shopping.

"That is a shame." He's standing behind me now, his hot breath making the hair on the back of my neck stand on edge.

"Do you want to come through the portal with me? We can sneak out and grab something at that new place by the palace or—"

His lips meet mine, and I feel every inch of his smile—among other things—as he leans into me. "I was hoping for sustenance of another kind," he says, his voice hoarse and hands rough as they grip my hips.

"Oh, thank god," I moan. He turns me so I'm facing him, our lips meeting with a feverish need. He was *so* writing something explicit up there in that loft. I hop up, using my wings for extra lift, and close my legs around his waist. He hoists me up onto the kitchen counter with ease.

"Comfortable?"

"Mmm," I purr, swinging my arms around his neck as I pull him in for the first of many "one last kisses." Light pours in from the windows, shining off the gold flecks of his skin. His eyes crease in half-moons and shine like gems before he slides onto his knees, moving my skirt out of the way, but my panties—

Snap.

The sound of the fabric ripping fills the kitchen, but it's not his claws doing the work, it's his teeth. He chews through the fabric until he gets to—

Oh my God. Each lick of his tongue sends shivers through my spine as he hits just the right spot. I squirm as my wings span out behind me, knocking into a few of the hanging pots and pans above the island that I make note to move in the future. Now, though, my toes curl as he grinds his mouth into me and oh—oh my God!

I moan, pulling him up to clamp my mouth down onto his shoulder, biting just the way I know he likes. We stay melted into each other for a long time, until finally, we find our way to the couch. Moth brews more coffee, and we pull a blanket over our tangled bodies. It's lovely and peaceful, and the perfect time to tell him the thought that's been building within me lately.

"You know, there's something I did want to talk about," I say. We've been in this house for a year and have been talking a lot about what the future holds. Moth is going to be an author and I'm so proud of him—and I love helping to run the studio.

"I keep walking past the spare rooms and thinking about what they'd look like … if they were different," I say, easing into the topic slowly.

"You know I trust your eye for decoration." He laughs, ruffling my hair. "Whatever you desire will be yours."

"I was thinking…" I shouldn't be nervous, we've talked about this so many times, but I finally feel like this is the moment. "A nursery?"

His hand combs up my thigh until it rests on my stomach. "Are you certain?" he asks, his eyes as wide as his smile.

"I'd need to set up an appointment to get my IUD removed—it's near its expiration date anyways, and we don't have to be in a rush, but yeah, I feel really, really sure." I hold tight to his arm. "I'll need bloodwork for my thyroid, and all the other stuff, but we wouldn't be able to officially start trying right away,"

With a mischievous grin, he picks me up and heads toward the bedroom. "Why not practice?"

Happiness rushes through me at the idea of what our future will hold. We will have a lifetime like this. Romance, laughter, sleeplessness, and too much coffee. Days will blur, seeming both long and short, in a house I hope is loud and filled with life.

I know that no matter what challenges we face, I'll be happy. In the shadows, in the sunshine, because like moth to a flame, we will always be together.

A letter to the Moth Court from the Vampire's Domain

Heather,

I understand that I must pay a penance, but do you think this is really necessary? My curtains are tattered, my court terrorized, and my bed has been taken over by this furry monstrosity. Of all the ways you could have retaliated, a cat? Claws and beak aside, you are more a monster than I could have given you credit for. A week has passed since your message arrived. Delivered by your sister-in-law, who I thought might stab me on arrival. She looked so satisfied while dropping the creature off, and I wondered if perhaps this was the peace offering I had been hoping for. Alas, the feline has decided to rage war with my linens and tapestries, and yet, I think I am growing fond of him all the same. I am still deciding on a name... Something smart, classic, fitting of the newest member of the Vampire Court.

I am thinking Mittens.

If you cannot tell by the rambly nature of this correspondence, I do miss you—terribly, if I'm being honest. Now that I am alone, I wish I had put more of an effort into the internet dating lessons you so generously offered. I have shamed my court, created controversy, and become the least desirable bachelor in Eclipsica. My only hope now is truly to get an unsuspecting mortal to swipe right. Perhaps then we can do that double date. If, of course, the two of you will have me.

Yours in unrequited friendship,
Magnus.

Thank you for enjoying this last chapter of Moth and Heather's story. It's truly been a pleasure to tell. Stay tuned for more adventures in Eclipsica with a swoon-worthy tale of a swamp monster. Join my mailing list on PaigeLavoie.com for all the newest updates and truly thank you for joining me on this adventure!

ACKNOWLEDGMENTS

OW. JUST WOW.
I can't even begin to thank you dear readers for the support I've felt while working on this series. I started Mothman in Love as a silly brief escape during the pandemic, and I truly think it's the most wonderful thing that the story I wrote just for fun has led me to all of you.

We've now gotten to hangout online and in person at signings, faerie picnics, and bookish balls, and I mean it when I say you are the most incredible group of readers EVER. Meeting you has been the highlight of my career. And I'm in awe seeing your tagged posts and cosplays; all of it has been surreal. It's amazing to see how talented you are, and I'm honored that, through the power of the internet and bookish events, I can call so many of you friends, which reminds me, happy birthday month, Katie!

I'm excited to share more stories with all of you in the future and can't wait to dive into some of the spin-offs of the characters you've met in the story! You know Gil will be getting his own book, but I have some plans for Magnus too... I'm so curious what you thought of our "Sad Pathetic Vampire." You'll have to let me know if you think he deserves a romance of his own because I think he's a villain worth redeeming.

We might even see Queen Plume again...

I love these characters so much, and it makes me so happy every time I hear that you have loved them too. I've gotten to know them all so well that writing this book felt like being at a party.

Thank you for venturing into this world of cryptids and faeries with me. You've truly brought pieces of this world alive in a way I never expected. I'm the luckiest author in the world because of your support, and I can't wait to hopefully see you soon at a signing or on social media! (the posts y'all tag me in literally make my day!)

I won't lie—while I was drafting this story, imposter syndrome was eating me up. It was just before the second book in the series came out, and I had absolutely overextended myself that year. I'd been dealing with burnout and a flair up similar to what we saw Heather have in the last book, and I think part of that made me feel even more in tune with her while I was writing this last part of the story. Our girl has been through a lot and tried to push all her feelings down, only to have them bubble up and really take a new form (literally!) here. It was fun to unravel some of her rage and have her stretch her wings and claws for a change.

I want to thank my beta-readers Bella, Kim, Kim B. and Selena for their incredible feedback and for cheering me on. Y'all read through the messiest version of this story and provided 10/10 feedback that I'm so grateful for. Thank you for your forgiveness with the wild level of typos and repeated paragraphs. Seriously… rockstars.

Thank you to my husband Matt for listening to me pace around the house talking about plot points, bringing me honey lattes, and making a detailed spreadsheet to help me stay organized (even though I forget to update it). You mean the world to me, and I appreciate the way you not only make space for me to create within our busy lives, you give the best feedback—and kisses.

Forever shutouts to Taylor, Meaghan, and Erin for their friendship, the ability to distract me from anxiety with adventures and tangents, and being some of the best travel and event buddies I could ask for. Also thank you Erin for all the brainstorm sessions and naming Clawece! It's so much cuter than the placeholder name "Muffin" I had for Gil's gator in the first draft of this story.

A big thank you to Lashes Lane for always being there when I have a deadline and being the best sister ever.

To 4 Horsemen Publications for their incredible support over the past few years. I still remember our first meeting when I talked through this campy Mothman romcom series and the way y'all believed in me 100% from the start. You've helped my books find new readers, and I'm so thankful for the wonderful community of authors I've met through us working together.

Beau and Jen are my editing heroes. Thank you for being such wonderful creatives, and teaching me that 'til is short for the word until… who knew?

LiyaDraws for always bringing Moth and Heather to life in illustration in the most beautiful way.

A big shoutout to the Orlando coffee scene for keeping me caffeinated with wonderful spaces to sip and write. I love our community here and maybe one day I'll write a story that takes place in one of them instead of off in the wilderness. Cryptids probably go to coffee shops too, right?

Eerie Travels for bringing my books to The Mothman Festival! The feeling of signing early copies of *I'm Engaged to Mothman* and sending them to y'all knowing they'd be in Point Pleasant was just the best, and I loved being tagged in readers' posts who found me at the event!

The book sellers who have stocked this series around the country and made my dreams come true. And the readers who make me want to write this pair forever. There will be more monsters in the future, and I hope you'll stick around to meet them. From the bottom of my heart, thank you for falling in love with Moth and Heather.

I'm so grateful to have you here.

BOOK CLUB QUESTIONS

1. What lessons do you think Heather learned during her character arc throughout the series?
2. Similarly, how do you feel Moth grew through each book?
3. Chris became the villain everyone loved to hate. Did you feel the same about Magnus?
4. Where would you take Magnus on a fake date in the mortal realm?
5. If you could add a song to the wedding reception playlist, what song would you pick?
6. How do you think Heather's early life as an internet star has affected her as an adult?
7. Who from the supporting cast of the *Mothman in Love* series would you like to learn more about?
8. After Chris left, do you think Moth ate the "offerings" he left outside the cabin?
9. Who would you rather read a spin off novel about, Gil or Magnus?
10. Do you have a favorite book in the *Mothman In Love* series?
11. What do you think Moth and Heather's future will look like in five years?

ABOUT THE AUTHOR

PAIGE LAVOIE IS A HALLOWEEN-loving cinnamon roll who writes stories about misfits, monsters, and falling in love. Her affection for cozy autumn moments, charming protagonists, and all things cute and creepy reflects in the worlds she creates. When Paige isn't writing, she can be found hunting for treasures at the local antique mall and sipping oat milk lattes under a lacy parasol as she hides from the sun in her home state of FL.

Discover more at
4HorsemenPublications.com

10% off using HORSEMEN10